Princess Academy

The Forgotten Sisters

ALSO BY SHANNON HALE

❧

THE BOOKS OF BAYERN
The Goose Girl
Enna Burning
River Secrets
Forest Born

❧

Princess Academy
Princess Academy: Palace of Stone

❧

Book of a Thousand Days

❧

Dangerous

❧

GRAPHIC NOVELS
with Dean Hale
illustrations by Nathan Hale
Rapunzel's Revenge
Calamity Jack

❧

FOR ADULTS
Austenland
Midnight in Austenland
The Actor and the Housewife

Princess Academy

The Forgotten Sisters

SHANNON HALE

BLOOMSBURY

NEW YORK   LONDON   NEW DELHI   SYDNEY

First published in the United States of America in March 2015
by Bloomsbury Children's Books
www.bloomsbury.com

Bloomsbury is a registered trademark of Bloomsbury Publishing Plc

For information about permission to reproduce selections from this book,
write to Permissions, Bloomsbury Children's Books,
1385 Broadway, New York, New York 10018
Bloomsbury books may be purchased for business or promotional use.
For information on bulk purchases please contact Macmillan Corporate and
Premium Sales Department at specialmarkets@macmillan.com

Library of Congress Cataloging-in-Publication Data
Hale, Shannon.
Princess Academy : the forgotten sisters / by Shannon Hale.
pages   cm
Summary: Miri is eager to return to her beloved Mount Eskel after a year
at the capital, but the king and queen ask her to first journey to a
distant swamp and start her own miniature princess academy for three
royal cousins, but once there she must solve a mystery before she can return home.
ISBN 978-1-61963-485-5 (hardcover) • ISBN 978-1-61963-486-2 (e-book)
[1. Princesses—Fiction.   2. Self-confidence—Fiction.   3. Kings, queens,
rulers, etc.—Fiction.   4. Telepathy—Fiction.   5. Mountains—Fiction.
6. Schools—Fiction.   7. Mystery and detective stories.]
I. Title.   II. Title: Forgotten sisters.
PZ7.H13824Prt 2015   [Fic]—dc23   2014013744

Book design by Donna Mark
Typeset by Westchester Book Composition
Printed and bound in the U.S.A. by Thomson-Shore Inc., Dexter, Michigan
4 6 8 10 9 7 5 3

All papers used by Bloomsbury Publishing, Inc., are natural, recyclable products
made from wood grown in well-managed forests. The manufacturing processes
conform to the environmental regulations of the country of origin.

For Ava & Shauna

And all golden friends

Princess Academy

THE FORGOTTEN SISTERS

Chapter One

The god of creation broke me from stone
The mountain's the only ma I've known
My pa is the blue sky sheltering me
So stone I am and sky I'll be

Miri woke to the rustle of a feather-stuffed quilt. She stretched, her muscles humming. Warm yellow light poured through the glass windows, filling the chamber with morning. For a moment she was not sure why her breath felt ticklish in her chest, as if she were at chapel and trying to hold in a laugh. Then she remembered. She was going home.

"Today," said Miri, her voice creaky with sleep.

Her roommates were awake too. A year ago, six Mount Eskel girls had come to Asland, Danland's capital city, for their friend Britta's marriage to Prince Steffan. Now four remained at the palace.

Esa dressed slowly, expertly using her right hand to pull her dress over her lame arm. Frid tore off her night things and stuffed her broad shoulders into a travel dress. Gerti, the youngest, just sat on the edge of her bed, her feet dangling.

"Today," said Gerti, and the word was both mournful and glad.

Their bags were already packed and fat with presents for their families. With her allowance as a lady of the princess, Miri had purchased a set of chapel clothes, paper and ink, and chocolates for her sister, Marda. For Pa she had boots, honeyed nuts, and a new mallet. For the village school, an entire box of precious books.

Palace servants offered to carry their bags, leaving the four girls free to hold hands as they walked through the grand corridors, perhaps for the last time.

"It's kind of like home now," Gerti said. A servant was carrying her lute, and Miri thought Gerti looked small and vulnerable without the instrument strapped in its usual place over her chest. "It's strange, isn't it? How we're leaving home to go home?"

"The boys at the forge tried to make me swear I'd come back." Frid laughed. "Asland is all right for a visit, but I'm a Mount Eskel girl."

"I think I'll visit again, one day," said Esa. As they passed the infirmary, she waved to the palace physicians who had spent the past months training her in their science.

Miri did not admit to the girls that she was already

planning to return next spring. After all, even her pa and her sister did not know yet. But she and Peder had agreed that there was too much to do and learn in Asland to say farewell forever.

Miri took in a deep breath, memorizing the smells of the palace—sunlight warming the oil and lemon polish, the lavender soap used on the linens, and the hard scent she associated with metal. Miri smiled. But at the moment, she yearned for linder dust, warm goats, the wind against the autumn grasses. All the welcome smells of home.

"First thing when we get to Mount Eskel," Frid said, "I'm going to throw a rock into the Great Crevasse."

"A big rock, no doubt," said Esa.

"As big a rock as I can lift. Ha! I can't wait."

Frid marched first out the doors and into the palace courtyard. Miri was last but hesitated only a moment before passing into the sunlight.

The traders' wagons were loaded with food and other supplies to sell to the families on Mount Eskel. One empty wagon waited for the girls. Peder was sharing the bench with the driver.

Beyond the palace gates, beyond the sea of green park, the colorful buildings of Asland rose like a range of mountains. Autumn had softened the heat of summer, but the buildings were painted bright—red, yellow, blue, white, rust, green—as if in the capital spring was end-less, always blooming, never cold.

The princess Britta, Miri's best friend, was waiting to see them off, standing beside her new husband, Prince Steffan. Britta lifted a hand to wave at Miri but wiped a tear instead. Her cheeks were bright red as always, that merry feature contrasting with her wet brown eyes.

Though they had spent every day of the past week together and already said good-bye in a hundred ways, Miri hugged Britta again. Britta's back shuddered with a small sob.

"Remember, Britta—" Miri started, trying to think of something funny to dull the sadness, but a man's voice interrupted.

"Miri Larendaughter?"

Miri turned. A royal guard in a shiny silver breast-plate and tall fur hat was striding across the courtyard.

"I'm Miri."

"The king requests your presence," he said.

Miri laughed nervously. "Right now? We're just leaving."

"The king requests your presence," the royal guard said again.

"What is this about?" asked Steffan. He stiffened to his full height, and his manner reminded Miri that a boy who grows up in a palace probably never truly relaxes.

The guard bowed, noticing the prince for the first time. "I don't know, Your Highness, but the king has also sent for you."

Britta hooked Miri's arm. "Fine, we'll see what's going on and be back in a few minutes."

"You'll wait for me?" Miri asked Enrik, their wagon driver.

He lifted his thin nose and sniffed, as if he could tell the time of day by smell. "If we want to reach the first camp before night, we have to go now."

Miri's middle felt yanked.

"On horseback you can easily catch up to a caravan of wagons," said Britta.

"That's right," said Steffan. "Even if my father delays you for a couple of hours, I could get you to the camp by tonight."

Peder jumped down from the wagon. "Then I'll stay with you."

The sun behind him, Peder's curly hair looked pale gold. This past year's apprenticeship with a stone carver had broadened his shoulders. His face and arms were brown from the summer, and to Miri, he looked as handsome as morning.

"But what if . . ." Miri cleared her throat. "What if I'm delayed longer?"

"All the more reason I should stay."

"You promised your pa you'd be home after a year. If you aren't on the first wagon, he'll be—"

"Grumpier than a hungry billy goat," finished Esa, Peder's sister.

"I don't want him mad at us, not now," said Miri. As soon as she and Peder got home to Mount Eskel, they were going to ask their parents to approve their betrothal.

Peder scowled, but he did not disagree.

"I'll find out what's happening," said Miri, "and then I'll catch up on a fast horse, like Britta said."

"I don't know about that," Peder said, "I have never actually seen you ride a fast horse."

"Steffan can strap me to the horse's rump like a sack of wheat."

Peder smiled. "These lowlanders sure know how to have fun."

Miri leaned in to hug him farewell, but Peder stopped her with a kiss.

Frid, Esa, and Gerti exclaimed and hooted. Miri's and Peder's affection for each other was not a secret, but they'd never announced their intentions to become betrothed and certainly never kissed in front of others. Miri's face burned forge-fire hot, but feeling stubborn, she put her arms around his neck and kissed him back.

"See you tonight," he said, still holding her.

She let go and felt colder without his arms. The cold creeped into her heart and pinched there, a sharp, unexpected loneliness.

She scolded herself for being silly. After all, surely she would see him by end of day.

Peder and the girls sat in the wagon backward, their faces turned toward Miri. She watched until their wagon had passed through the gate and disappeared into the streets of Asland.

"Now, if you please," said the royal guard.

As they made their way to the royal breakfast chamber, Miri's sadness simmered into anger, her hands tightening into fists. She prepared herself to be bold and speak frankly with the king about her sudden summons. But then she entered the chamber and breathed in the icy, tense mood. With the king sat all thirty-two delegates, an elected noble and a commoner from each province in the kingdom. Three priests of the creator god stood along the wall in their brown tunics and white caps. Everyone wore equally grave expressions. The queen's gaze found Miri, and her smile seemed relieved.

"Your Highness," Britta said after the guard formally announced them, "Lady Miri was about to return to Mount Eskel when your summons prevented her."

"And is my summons not good enough anymore?"

The king's beard shook as his chin trembled. "Does the wish of the king mean nothing?"

Britta blushed, her entire face turning as red as her mottled cheeks. For the first time that morning, Miri thought to be afraid.

"Father—" Steffan began.

The king waved his hand dismissively and gestured to the chief delegate, a thin man with a small, pointed beard.

"Early this morning, traders sailed from the commonwealth of Eris with news," said the chief delegate. "The kingdom of Stora has invaded Eris. The battle lasted only three days. Eris surrendered."

Steffan leaned forward to grip a chair back. Britta reached out for Miri's hand. Stora was the largest kingdom on the continent. Miri imagined its vast army pouring into tiny Eris like all the sands of a beach trying to fill a single jar. And Eris bordered Danland.

"Danland can no longer take for granted our longstanding peace with Stora," the chief delegate continued. "We must secure an unbreakable alliance. Stora's King Fader is a widower. The delegation has decided to offer King Fader a royal daughter of Danland as a bride."

"Ironic, isn't it?" said the king, clattering plates as he reached for a bread basket. "Commoners clamor for revolution and the end of royal rule. But the moment the neighbors start loading their muskets, everyone runs to the king crying, 'Save us!' I have half a mind to let Stora invade and slaughter a province or two before coming to their aid."

"But you won't, sire," said the queen.

"Of course I won't," he barked back.

The queen nodded and sipped her tea. She was a pale woman with dark hair and strong features whose beauty seemed excessive whenever she uncurled a rare smile.

"An alliance through marriage is often strongest," said the chief delegate. "We have been neglectful of making such a union in the past because the queen bore no daughters."

Queen Sabet dropped her teacup onto the saucer with a loud *clank*. The king placed a hand on her arm.

"The highest-ranking royal girls are His Majesty's cousins," said the chief delegate. "They live in a territory known as Lesser Alva. Three girls. King Fader of Stora will have his pick of them for a bride, if he agrees to our offer."

"I wonder if the girls will have any say in the matter," Steffan said, speaking the question on Miri's mind.

"Royalty has its obligations," said the chief delegate.

Steffan nodded, and Miri noticed his shoulders slump slightly.

"Living in Lesser Alva, I suspect the girls are not very, shall we say, *refined*," said the chief delegate. "The priests of the creator god have called for a princess academy to prepare them, and the delegation approved it. We require this girl to go be their tutor." He gestured toward Miri without looking at her.

Miri choked. "Me? But I . . . I can't . . . I'm going . . ."

The king turned to his wife. "She can barely speak. Are you certain?"

"I am," said the queen, her gaze on her spilled tea.

"Yes, of course, she is the best choice," he said.

"I've completed only one year of study at the Queen's Castle," said Miri. "It takes four years to become a tutor."

"Make her one, Bjorn," said the queen.

The king waved his napkin. "Chief, sign some paper that makes Miri a tutor."

"Yes, Your Majesty," said the chief delegate.

Miri looked at Britta, Steffan, the delegates, searching for someone who thought this idea was as ridiculous as she did. "But why me? There are lots of real tutors—"

"According to our traditions and the dictates of the priests, a tutor for a princess academy must be a princess academy graduate herself," said the chief delegate.

"A more experienced tutor—" Miri started.

"I don't know anyone else," said the queen. "I know you. Please."

"You don't need to say 'please,'" the king roared. "You tell her to go, and she will go."

"*I* have no choice?" asked Miri.

The king shifted in his seat and glared at the chief delegate from under his thick eyebrows.

"She does have a choice," the chief delegate said reluctantly.

Miri opened her mouth to decline so she could hurry and catch up with Peder, but she paused. Would the king be angry and forbid Steffan from escorting her to the camp? No other trader wagons would trek to Mount Eskel until next spring. How could she catch up without the king's permission?

Lesser Alva. She'd read about the outer territory, but at the moment all she could remember was one word: "swamp." The queen and king were ordering her to a swamp to be a teacher to his cousins? She'd been in Asland for a year, and with every letter home, she'd promised Marda and Pa she would return in the fall.

She felt Britta step closer, her shoulder touching Miri's, a faint warmth of encouragement.

"I need to think about it," Miri said.

The chief delegate took a breath to shout, but the king lifted his hand.

"Give her a little time," he grumbled into his beard. "She deserves that much."

The chief delegate pulled Steffan and the king into renewed talk about Stora.

Miri's breath felt tight, as if the walls were pressing in, squeezing. The king's voice begin to sound tinny and high-pitched, as far away as an echo. Miri opened the door and slipped out.

Chapter Two

I spy a dull stone
Smartly hidden in scree
Now small and unknown
Soon polished you will be
Carved into a throne
In a castle by the sea

Miri's legs shook, and she imagined she would feel stronger if she just ran. She could run down the corridor, through the courtyard, and into the streets of Asland. Run somehow fast enough to catch up with the wagons. Maybe just run all the way home.

Before she even took a step, the breakfast chamber door opened. Miri expected to see Britta, but it was Katar, Mount Eskel's first delegate to the court in Asland. She was a little older than Miri and a lot taller, with hair so red it seemed angry.

"I don't want—" Miri broke off. She hid her quivering chin with a hand.

"Oh stop it," said Katar. "They're not asking you to cut off your head."

Miri nodded, staying silent to keep the sob in her chest from unsticking.

"Danland needs the stronger alliance a marriage with Stora's king would give us," Katar said. "If Stora invades and defeats Danland's army, then all the changes we worked for—commoner delegates, justice and equality for all Danlanders—all of it will be just *undone*."

Miri nodded again. Katar was right, and yet the loneliness that had pricked her heart when the wagons rolled away without her was spreading outward, chilling her legs and arms.

Katar rubbed her own arms. "It's important, Miri. It's really important. Go, and don't mess it up."

Now Miri felt sick as well as sad.

"There's something else you should know." Katar sighed. "Even though Mount Eskel was made a province, the king still owns all the land. Well, now the chief delegate is encouraging the king to sell his rights to the land to merchants in order to replenish the royal treasury."

"Sell? He couldn't—"

"He could," said Katar. "Merchants would pay the king well for the rights to mine and sell linder. They would move up to Mount Eskel and oversee the quarry."

"Then the Eskelites would work for the merchants, not for ourselves," said Miri.

"Exactly. And the merchants could bring up new workers and fire the villagers, set wages lower than what our people are making now, and really do whatever they please."

"Mount Eskel wouldn't be a town anymore," said Miri. "It would just be a mine. You can't let them."

"I explained that there's no other means of survival on Mount Eskel besides quarrying, so if the merchants fired any Eskelites, we'd have to leave our homes. But the king imagines the Eskelites would be grateful for the chance to move to the lowlands, where *surely* they'd all be *much* happier."

Miri felt tired. They'd fought so hard to improve life on the mountain, and then fought to get commoners in the delegation and improve life in the kingdom, but there was always another fight.

"Miri," said Katar, "you need—"

"I know," Miri said. "I *know*. But right now I need to be alone."

She walked away.

First Miri went back to the chamber where she and the other Mount Eskel girls had slept for the past year. The wardrobes were empty, doors ajar. All her things were packed and bouncing around in the back of a wagon on its way to Mount Eskel. All she had was the hawk Peder had carved for her out of linder stone, a familiar weight in her pocket.

Servants and guards knew Miri, and she wandered freely through the white stone palace as she had always done. The linder stone beneath her feet was as white as cream, with pale green veins, quarried from Mount Eskel generations before. Miri had grown up climbing on rough blocks of linder, breathing linder dust, and drinking from a stream white with it. But the beauty of polished linder still filled her with awe.

She climbed stairs until she reached the top floor and a balcony facing north. She could not see Mount Eskel all the way from Asland, just a hint of purple mountains far against the horizon. The wagons would be miles away by now and take days more to reach the mountain pass.

Dozens of times she had imagined her return—embracing Pa and Marda, giving them her carefully chosen gifts. If she agreed to accept the king's errand, Peder would deliver the gifts with the message that Miri was not coming yet. Despite the new boots and chocolates, there would be no joy beside their little hearth.

"I'm not going home." She whispered the words aloud to convince herself they were true.

She sat down, stared north, and let the minutes ride away from her like Peder in the wagon.

Royals aren't the only ones with obligations. She thought the words hard, as if they were stones she could throw at the chief delegate.

She was in the palace library reading about tutorships when she heard quarry-speech—not heard so much as felt, a vibration that entered her and created an idea in her mind. On Mount Eskel, quarry workers used quarry-speech to communicate warnings and instructions, when deafening mallet blows made it impossible to hear normal talk. Miri had discovered that quarry-speech traveled only through linder stone and communicated through memories. The quarry-speech entering her now had the sense of Katar about it and prompted a memory of playing hide-and-find-me as a child. With that memory, Katar was asking Miri, *Where are you?*

Miri knocked on the linder in imitation of the quarry workers' mallet blows and sang a work song. "I spy a dull stone smartly hidden in scree." Though it was not necessary, singing aloud helped her focus. Quarry-speech had a rhythm to it, and was more like a silent song than simple thoughts. By quarry-speaking a memory of an afternoon she and Katar had spent in the library, Miri was letting Katar know where to find her.

Katar must have reported to Britta where Miri was, because a few minutes later, Britta plopped down on the couch beside her.

"Not too great a day, is it?" Britta said.

"I don't know what you mean," said Miri, her voice croaking after so much silence. "I'm having the best time ever. Let's do it again tomorrow."

"I could arrange a mass public execution for your pleasure," Britta said in a stiff, high voice, as if pretending to be an official.

"That would be lovely," Miri replied in a warbling tone. "And perhaps the physician could entertain me by pulling out all my teeth."

"I'll see to it at once, my lady."

They leaned against each other, Miri's head on Britta's shoulder.

"I was too excited to eat breakfast and too sick to eat lunch," said Miri. "I'd go find some dinner, but the way this day is going, I'm afraid the kitchen is serving something like mud and frogs."

"The kitchen served mud and frogs yesterday," Britta said. "Tonight we're dining on your teeth."

Miri tightened her belly to encourage a laugh, but she could not quite muster it.

"I want to go home," she whispered.

"I know," Britta whispered back. "Selfishly I want you

in Asland with me. But this—Lesser Alva, cousins, a princess academy?"

A servant came to fetch them, and they followed him to the king's personal dining chamber.

"I thought we'd be more comfortable in here," said the king.

Miri took in the gilded chairs and porcelain dishes in a room that could hold three village houses and suddenly found it easy to laugh.

The king raised an eyebrow.

"Sorry, I wasn't laughing at you, sire," she said.

"Of course you weren't," he said, his attention returning to his food. "And that is why you are still standing before me and not dragged away to the dungeon."

"Oh Bjorn," the queen whispered. "Please don't upset her now."

The queen especially seemed to want Miri and no other tutor. Miri had learned during her own time at a princess academy that when people desire something that is in short supply, it is worth more.

She cleared her throat. "I will go to Lesser Alva if, instead of giving me a tutor's wages, you sign over the land of Mount Eskel."

For the first time that day, the chief delegate looked directly at Miri.

"When I and the other girls graduated from the

princess academy on Mount Eskel, we were made ladies of the princess, a noble title," said Miri. "I read that when commoners are granted noble titles, they are traditionally given lands tied to their titles—"

The chief delegate interrupted, "It's been a hundred years or more since—"

"When we were made ladies of the princess, we became the only nobility in the entire kingdom who don't own land," Miri continued, her voice louder. "I'm not asking much, just that the ladies of the princess become the owners and caretakers of the village and quarry."

The chief delegate laughed. "She doesn't ask much?"

"These are my terms," Miri said, her voice weakening.

"Give it to her," said the queen.

"Not the quarry," said the king.

"Give it to her," the queen repeated.

The king harrumphed. "If she completes her tutorship, the land under her village is theirs. If she completes her tutorship *well* and King Fader marries one of the girls in an alliance of peace, then the quarry is theirs."

Miri did not feel any better. The idea of home, so vibrant just that morning, as large and hot as the sun, had dimmed, pulling back into a faint prick of a star.

"Very well," Miri said. "I'll go."

The queen sighed as if she'd been holding her breath.

Miri asked for parchment and ink to write a letter to Peder explaining about the king's cousins and the swamp princess academy, as well as the king's plan to sell Mount Eskel, so Peder would understand Miri did not take up this duty thoughtlessly.

The king commanded one of the royal guards to take the letter to the camp, and he left at once. Miri hooked her ankles around her chair legs to keep from running after him.

The chief delegate talked at her through all seven courses of the meal.

"It is not your place to tell the girls about their future," he said. "Prepare them to behave like princesses. Enrich their minds, polish their behavior. When we bring them to Asland next spring, King Bjorn himself will inform his cousins about their possible marriage to King Fader. Do you understand?"

Miri had a mouthful of buttered squash, but she nodded.

"You will remain in Lesser Alva through the winter at least," said the chief delegate. "We do not want them seen in Asland until you have polished them. We cannot afford the chance some nosy courtier might witness their uncivilized behavior. Gossip can travel all the way to Stora."

The moment the king finished the cheese and cherries course, the chief delegate arose.

"A ship sails west at midnight," said the chief delegate. "You will be on it."

Since Miri's things were long gone, Britta packed some of her own clothing for Miri. The kitchen provided a hamper of food. Steffan pressed a small bag of coins into her hand.

"Thanks," said Miri. She hugged him impulsively and felt for a moment how life might be different with an older brother.

"My father was king because his older brother died," said Steffan. "I will be king because I am the only child of my father. Some matters happen by chance. But you, Miri, are not a tutor by chance."

"If only I'd tried to be a little less remarkable," she said, trying to smile.

"Duty doesn't always fit comfortably." He mimed screwing an invisible crown onto his head, squinting as if it pinched.

"Britta did not choose you by chance. And I approve."

The chief delegate snatched the coin bag from Miri. "Prince Steffan, his highness your father sends a generous monthly allowance to his cousins in Lesser Alva. You are very kind, but Lady Miri will not need money."

The moon lingered over the courtyard, almost full and yet so high up it appeared small, no bigger than the print of her pinky finger on glass. Miri stood under the moon, making farewells. Katar gave Miri a fierce hug and ran off. Britta kissed Miri's cheeks and made promises of letters. The king and queen did not come out at all. Steffan apologized on behalf of his mother, saying that she was unwell.

Miri felt courageous as she stepped into the carriage, a warrior off to some unknown battle.

Courage is not fearlessness, Master Filippus, her tutor at the Queen's Castle, had taught. *Courage is feeling justly afraid and yet still doing what is right.*

Was she doing what was right?

She leaned out the carriage window to wave goodbye. Steffan bowed to her, Britta called out luck, and the pinky print of the moon hovered, indifferent in the blackness above.

Chapter Three

~~~~~~~~~

A honey bee, a funny flea, a pitter patter sunny sea
A breezy snow, a wheezy crow, a bitter batter easy dough
A teary hymn, a weary limb, a titter tatter cheery swim
A cozy yawn, a nosy fawn, a chitter chatter rosy dawn

Miri spent four days aboard the ship. Brief sails around Asland's harbor had not prepared her for the open sea. Now she learned that waves could crest white, a ship could fly and fall, and novice passengers were rightly called "green."

The captain was stout and lively, and advised her to stay up in the open and ride the sickness out. The sky and wind felt as firm as solid ground above her head, and by the second day she could look away from the horizon without fearing she'd have to revisit her breakfast. Without sickness to distract her thoughts, worry and dread swooped in. She sat alone, singing nonsense songs against the wind. "Salty sea and bunnies three, nothing like a honey tea, so fitter fatter, it don't matter, mind the chatter, scatter me."

Two royal guards accompanied her—one a thin, trim young man who smiled a great deal, the other balding and dark-eyed. They spoke to each other but rarely to her.

The first time the ship stopped at a port to unload cargo from Asland and load new goods, Miri lent a hand, making the sailors laugh. Apparently noble passengers did not usually engage in merchant work, but Miri was weary of working over her own thoughts.

Soon she was learning to tie knots and climb ropes and trading stories and songs. Miri's stories were often historical accounts of famous Danlandians. The sailors' tales involved ports and women and made Miri blush, but she supposed they increased her education in one neglected area.

The last stop on their route was Greater Alva, and by then Miri and the captain spent hours each day talking and laughing.

"There's no port in Lesser Alva," the captain explained. "Too boggy. So I'll only be able to take you as far as Greater Alva. We rarely come all this way to trade, but when the king asks . . ." He saluted nobly.

"I knew a merchant shipman's son once," said Miri. "Timon Skarpson."

She had not thought his name in so many months that speaking it felt strange in her mouth.

"This is his ship," said the captain.

"This is Timon's?" Miri looked around, suddenly afraid he might appear.

"Actually, he was going to be on this voyage," said the captain, "but when we received the order to transport you, he decided to stay ashore. He said you two had a troubled history and you might be uncomfortable trapped aboard together."

"That was gentlemanly of him," she said. "And he was right. But would you carry a message? Just let him know that all is forgiven and I hope he's well."

The captain squinted. "I don't detect a broken heart about you, and certainly you have a love you left behind, given how often you hold that stone hawk of yours. My guess is Timon behaved badly and so missed out on being the one to give you a gift you would treasure as much as that hawk. A shame for his sake."

Miri felt like blushing but laughed instead.

In Greater Alva's harbor only a few fishing boats bobbed. Miri went ashore, immediately suspicious of the ground that neither rose nor fell. Her legs had gotten used to the motion of the sea and now refused to appreciate firm earth.

The port city was considerably smaller than Asland and smelled of fish. She ate lunch with the royal guards at the dockside tavern, her stomach too nervous to enjoy the salty fish stew. They hired an open carriage to take them out of town and a few hours through fields of wheat and barley. At the mouth of a scrubby forest, the wheel ruts of the road stopped.

"We walk the rest of the way," said one of her guards, shouldering her pack.

The farther they walked, the narrower the road became, until the thin, branchy trees tapped Miri's shoulders and touched overhead. The ground was spongy. The air was close. Miri wiped her forehead with her sleeve.

Astrid, Felissa, and Susanna. Miri thought the names of the royal cousins over and over again, from oldest to youngest. They seemed to be just words, not names. She could not imagine faces to match, let alone a palace in a swamp, or even a swamp at all. Nothing seemed quite real. It was as if she were walking through the landscape of a dream.

Miri was no tutor, no matter that the king had signed a paper saying so. Her instructor at the princess academy, Tutor Olana, had been a grown woman, smart and well-read, and as scary as a viper in a basket.

Miri was short, young, and undereducated. She must appear as imposing as Tutor Olana had been, or the royal cousins would never respect her. Miri would walk into Lesser Alva with head high, shoulders back, eyes glinting with secret knowledge, voice firm and commanding.

Astrid. Felissa. Susanna.

The trees finally petered out. Miri took a deep breath—and coughed. The air was even thicker here than in the woods, wet and muggy and full of rotting things. Sweat pricked her skin.

From the edge of the woods, the ground sloped down. Sunlight glinted off mud and water. A wide, slow river ended in a marshy lake, twinkling between rising arms of land. Miri knew from maps that the water eventually joined an inlet of the sea. Straight ahead, a village sat on an island in the middle of the sludgy water. All the houses were built of dried reeds.

The water was busy with two-person boats—long and narrow, made of tightly bound bundles of reeds. The person in the bow of each boat held a barb-tipped spear, punting with the flat end in the water. The person behind held a long-poled net. They were fishing. Or hunting, Miri supposed.

Far off to the right on a solitary patch of high, dry ground, looking like a porcelain cup in a pig sty, stood a small cube of a house built entirely of linder.

"Lesser Alva," said the older of the guards. "Well, good luck."

He put down Miri's pack and turned to go.

"Wait!" she said. "You're not staying?"

"Our orders were to deliver you safely to Lesser Alva," he said as he walked away. "The royal cousins live in the white stone house. The servants of their house will take care of you. We need to reach Greater Alva before dark if we're to make the ship back."

"But . . ." Miri followed after them, clutching her hands. "But don't you want to stay the night? At least?"

"I don't like snakes," the younger guard said apologetically. He flashed a helpful smile before disappearing into the trees.

Miri stood listening to the sounds of the guards walking away, leaves flapping, branches snapping. The sounds stopped. And then started again. Were they returning after all? Hope flared like a burn against her heart. But instead of returning guards, a small brown animal emerged, scurrying right across her foot. She stifled a scream and turned around.

People had gathered from the village to watch her. Surprised, she slipped and fell on her backside. Mud seeped through her skirt and leggings. The crowd was mostly children, and they kept staring.

"You don't look like a trader," said one child.

"No, I'm just . . . going over there," Miri said, pointing

to the linder house. She grabbed her pack and stumbled away.

Chickens ran loose, clucking with annoyance and attacking insects that had the gall to hide beneath dead leaves. A flock of thin, long-necked birds flew off the water, settling on a shore. Against the deep brown and green background, their bright whiteness looked as startling in that setting as the linder house.

The sunlight on the water flashed and glared. Miri squinted, her head pounding. The straps of her pack cut into her shoulders. The ground was slippery, her boot soles thick with mud. She could not spare a hand to wipe the sweat dripping onto her cheeks.

You are a tutor, she told herself. *You have to be imposing!*

The wooden door in its frame looked swollen and misshapen, though perhaps years ago it had fit properly in the cut stone. It swung inward at her first knock, squeaking on its hinges.

"Hello?" Miri called out. She stepped inside.

The building was only one room, and it was nearly empty. The polished stone floor tilted to one side, some stones jutting higher than others, as if over the years the ground had settled.

"Who's there?"

A girl was climbing in through one of the open

windows, followed by two others. They wore loose brown shirts and leggings, stained even browner up to the knees, and held sticks and poles.

"Who are you? What are you doing in our house?" asked the tallest one.

In their house? These wild girls were the royal cousins? Miri guessed the tall one was Astrid, the eldest girl.

"Call the village," the middle one whispered—probably Felissa.

"She doesn't look like a bandit," said the shortest. Susanna.

Miri worked her tongue in her mouth, but it was so dry. They would notice how young she was, and her short stature made her seem even younger. They would see she was a fraud and not a real tutor at all. She had to be strong, speak firmly, demand respect. Be imposing.

"I am your tutor. You may call me Tutor Miri."

"Who?" asked Astrid.

"You should raise your hand if you . . . when you want to talk . . . or ask something. Though I may not answer. Immediately."

The girls looked at one another, baffled. Miri's head felt funny, her legs kind of tingly, but if she sat, she would seem weak.

Astrid raised her hand and said, "You're in our house."

Miri looked around. "There aren't any books. I don't see a single book."

"I don't see a single snake in here either," said Astrid. "I don't see a single lot of things. *Who* are you?"

"I only brought three books because I thought . . ." Her head felt as tilty as the floor. "There's no furniture either. Why do you live here? You're the king's cousins. You're royalty."

"So we've heard," Astrid said and stepped in front of her younger sisters, still gripping her long, sharpened stick.

"I'm feeling a little . . . muddled. There was a long walk and so hot and the ground's still leaning as if it wants to be water—" Miri giggled. "I sound crazy, don't I? I don't mean to. I'm just . . . thirsty . . ."

Miri watched the floor swell like a white ocean, leisurely, pleasantly. Her limbs felt wonderfully light, and she sighed right before the floor rose up to meet her.

It was dark out when Miri woke, coughing. Her face was wet, and water was dripping down her neck.

Felissa was crouching nearby, a cup in her hands, apparently having tried to give Miri a drink. Felissa offered the cup. Miri took it and gulped down the water, grateful despite its weedy flavor.

"You walked from Greater Alva without drinking enough water, didn't you?" Felissa asked, smiling.

Miri nodded.

"Why did you do a dumb thing like that?" asked Astrid.

"Well, I've never walked from Greater Alva to Lesser Alva before," said Miri. She felt she had to speak loudly in order to push her words past her headache. "You should post signs: 'Danger: this place is hotter than you expect.'"

"City folk," Astrid whispered to Felissa. Felissa smiled.

Miri was not sure of their ages. Susanna looked about ten but Astrid was likely a few years older than Miri. The chief delegate had not mentioned Miri would have to teach a girl older than she was.

Imposing?

She sat up and patted her head, feeling how her hair was springing loose from her braid. She straightened her shoulders.

"I'm Miri Larendaughter of Mount Eskel. His Majesty King Bjorn sent me here to be your tutor."

Susanna did not blink. Her face was as quiet and serious as Felissa's was constantly amused. "You said that word before. *Tutor*. What is a tutor?"

Felissa giggled. "Sounds like something you do after eating too much pig grass."

"A tutor is a *teacher*," Miri said quickly. "I can teach you Reading and Arithmetic and History, all kinds of subjects, even Poise."

"Why would we ever need to do those things?" Astrid asked. She was still standing by the window, the sharpened stick in her hand.

"Because . . . because . . ." Miri's head felt pressed between stones. Suddenly in that dark, strange little house, nothing that had happened in Asland made any sense at all. "Can we talk about this in the morning?"

"After breaking into our house, you're expecting us to let you stay?" said Astrid.

Miri blinked and had a hard time opening her eyes again. "Please," she whispered.

Felissa offered her a reed mat. Miri curled up on her side, using her pack of clothing as a pillow. She was too tired and dizzy to change out of her mud-splattered clothing. She barely managed to kick off her boots.

Imposing, Miri thought. She closed her eyes, and sleep came up to meet her, as hard as the floor.

Chapter Four

⟨⟨⟨⟨⟩⟩⟩⟩

Mouth curved and smiling
Head sleek and rounded
Its bite just a bee's sting
Your screams are unfounded

Head like an arrow
Body striped or stippled
Run from this slinker
Or it will leave you crippled

Morning buzzed and cawed and croaked. Miri swatted a fly from her face and sat up, groaning. The three girls were rolling up their reed mats, so Miri did the same.

"I'm sorry I didn't start with an introduction," she said. "I'd love to learn your names properly."

"See? I told you she'd ask eventually," Felissa said to Astrid.

"We weren't sure you had learned manners," said Susanna. "Folk from Asland can be bossy rude."

Miri felt her face burn. "Imposing" had been a bad idea.

At her princess academy, she'd studied the rules of Conversation, including finding common ground with others.

"I'm not from Asland, though I've been living there recently. I'm from a place called Mount Eskel. In fact, linder—these stones of your house—they were actually cut out of Mount Eskel itself!"

The girls stared back. Astrid, seeming to realize Miri expected a reaction to that news, said, "Oh."

Miri felt her shoulders slump. She cleared her throat. "So, what are your names?"

She'd guessed correctly, the tallest was also the oldest. Astrid was very thin, her brown hair loose and matted. Her nose was sharp, but her gaze was even sharper.

Next was Felissa. She had dark eyes like Astrid but paler hair, shiny as honey. Though she was thin like her sister, her cheeks were full, making her seem a healthy plump. She was almost always smiling, which put dimples in those cheeks.

The youngest, Susanna, introduced herself as just Sus. She was the same height as Miri, though she appeared to be only about ten years old. Whereas Felissa rarely stopped smiling, Sus did not seem to know how to start. She had dark hair, kinky with natural curls, and a gaze that was lazy without being dull.

"Where is everyone else?" Miri asked. "Servants? Guards? Your parents?"

Astrid stiffened. "It's just us," she said.

Miri shut her eyes. The royal guards were sailing back toward Asland by now. Asland, where a king and his ministers believed the royal cousins were outfitted with guards and servants and wealth. But whatever had happened to change that, Astrid clearly did not want to talk about it.

"Just so you know," said Felissa, her smile a little timid now, "in Lesser Alva one never, ever enters someone else's house without being invited."

"Never," Sus said, unblinking.

"Never ever," said Felissa, nodding.

"In fact, we could have killed you on the spot and cut you up for meat," Astrid said, casually cleaning out her fingernails.

"No one's ever really done that," said Sus.

"As far as we know," said Astrid. "But we *could* be the first and no one would stop us."

"I see." So as her very first act as their tutor, Miri had trampled on some sacred swamp custom. "I'm sorry.

The king ordered me to stay with you. Does that count?"

Astrid leaned forward, her stare hardening. "Do you see him living here?"

"Oh! Well, no. I mean, my duty is to stay with you for a while," said Miri, searching through her pack. "The king sent a letter."

She offered Astrid the king's signed and sealed letter, only slightly crumpled. Astrid opened it and looked it over, nodding. She was holding it upside down.

"Did you bring us things?" Sus asked, crouching beside Miri's pack. "City food?"

"Sus," said Felissa.

"I . . . um . . ." Miri rummaged through her things. She had three books, a stack of parchment, quills and ink, her sewing kit, and several of Britta's dresses. She found half of a sea biscuit and offered it to Sus.

The young girl held it between two fingers and licked a corner. "It tastes like dirt."

"And how would you know?" Felissa said, putting her fists on her hips. "You eat dirt often, do you? Snacking on mud pies when our backs are turned?"

"It tastes how dirt *smells*," Sus said.

"*You* smell," Felissa said, which would have seemed rude if she had not still been smiling.

Miri glanced over the house, white and empty as an eggshell. "I'm sorry I didn't bring more. I thought you'd have plenty."

"We do all right," Astrid said, standing up straighter.

"I'm sure you do," Miri said. There she went again, offending them. "Um . . . can I help you get breakfast ready?"

Astrid shrugged. "I guess."

The girls started for the door, so Miri did not change clothes, just brushed at the dried mud on her skirt and shoved on her boots.

Felissa pointed at Miri's feet. "What are those for?"

"My boots? Well, boots are like shoes but, um, taller."

Felissa laughed, her honey-yellow hair swaying. "I know what boots are, you muskrat! I meant, why in all creation did you put them on right before—"

"Just let her wear them," said Astrid.

Miri glanced at the girls' bare and filthy feet. Perhaps they'd never had boots of their own.

"Felissa, would you like to wear my boots?" Miri asked, starting to unlace them.

Felissa's laughter broke even higher. So Miri shrugged, laced them back up, and followed the girls out.

Apparently breakfast was not waiting for them in

some kitchen hut out back. Breakfast had to be hunted. They tromped away from the house and into a reed forest—thick, sturdy grass reaching well above Miri's head. Two herons flapped away on flat wings, long legs trailing. Astrid swung a pole at them but missed. Underfoot Miri crushed mint and pondweed, and then suddenly, ground that had looked solid swallowed Miri to her knees. Water and mud filled her boots, and her feet felt as heavy as boulders.

As soon as they reached a rare dry spot, Miri pulled off the sopping boots and, tying them by the laces, hung them around her neck, where they dripped muddy water on her clothes.

Sus whispered something, and Felissa giggled.

"Why do you live here?" Miri asked, trying to tiptoe through a muddy area without slipping.

"We were born here," Astrid said in her are-you-brainless voice.

"But you're royalty," said Miri. "Did you know that only royalty can live in a linder house? How did you end up here?"

"I think someone was naughty," Sus said, watching Miri with her intense, pale-eyed stare. "Maybe our ma's parents or grandparents made a king mad and the family was sent far away."

"Or maybe they *chose* to live here," said Astrid. A

mosquito lit on her cheek. She slapped it, leaving a tiny splatter of blood.

The girls checked traps. Some were knots of tough reeds woven together around a brace of thin branches, others were simple but clever snares. All were empty.

"Toad toots," Astrid said under her breath.

Miri supposed it was a local curse. She learned several more that morning: peat head, grouse kin, soggy bottom bellows, and stones.

As they approached a pond's edge, a trio of floating birds dived headfirst into the water. Miri watched but they did not come back up. In a swamp, the whole world seemed upside down. Next would fish take to the sky?

Felissa clambered thigh-deep in the stagnant water and began dragging a coarse net through its depths. Occasionally she snagged a few thumb-size fish and tossed them back to Sus.

"Got something!" Astrid shouted from nearby. A fat, brown swamp rat flailed, its neck caught in a trap. Astrid pulled a small knife out of her belt and stabbed it through the back of its head. She tucked the limp rat under her belt and set the trap back up.

Miri shivered and tried to hide it by joining Felissa in the pond.

"Here, I can try that," she offered.

The chill water crept up to her legs, her skirt spread out on top of the water like a lily pad. Suddenly her skirt jumped and twitched as if something was caught beneath it. Miri lifted it, looking.

A strike of pain hit like a knife in her leg. Her hands went to her thigh, and she felt something hard and slick. It quivered away, skimming atop the water's surface. It was long and thin and shiny, thick as her wrist, built of dark brown scales. A snake.

Miri screamed. Her bare feet slipped on the pond bottom and she went under.

Felissa pulled her back up by her hair. Miri gasped and thrashed, fighting her way up the slimy bank and onto the muddy ground. She lay down, coughing and clutching at her leg. Her whole body vibrated, and she seemed to feel venom streak like heat from the wound through her veins. She was dying in a swamp. She'd never see home again.

"Let me see," Felissa said, prying Miri's hands away from her leg.

Felissa wiped the blood with her skirt and exposed a mark made of many small pricks in the shape of a horseshoe.

"Oh good," said Felissa.

Good? Were these girls insane? She'd been bitten by a swamp snake!

"You'll be fine," said Astrid. "If it'd been poisonous, you'd have just two teeth marks."

Astrid put her pointer fingers beside her mouth to mimic fangs.

Miri's panicked breathing still racked her chest, and blood oozed from her thigh, but the burn of venom she'd felt certain was coursing through her seemed to dim and fade.

"I guess you better go change," said Astrid. "Think you can find your way back?"

The white stone house was visible on the rise, clear as the sun.

"I think I can guess the general direction," Miri muttered.

"Then you have permission to enter our house."

Miri sloshed to her feet and stumbled away. Her wet skirt clung to her legs, sticky as a spider's web. Behind her, she could hear Astrid mutter, "City folk."

A rain barrel outside the house was nearly full. Miri stripped down to nothing, the house between her and the island village. She ladled some water over herself, scrubbing furiously at the mud and hesitantly at her leg wound. She tore a length from her shirt, pulled up some dry-ish moss, pressed it over the snake's bite, and wrapped her leg with the fabric to hold it there. The bleeding slowed.

She went inside and opened her pack, sorting for the first time through the clothes Britta had sent. And then she slumped to the floor, her face in her hands. Britta had packed her own wardrobe for Miri. A princess's wardrobe.

When the girls returned, Miri was wearing a yellow silk dress, belted and pulled to keep from dragging on the floor. Astrid snorted.

"How's your leg?" Felissa asked, pretending not to notice her ridiculous attire.

Miri shrugged as if she were not bothered a bit, but she could not help shuddering.

"If you jump into the water in a skirt, flailing and backing up every which way, you're going to get bit," said Astrid.

Felissa crouched by Miri, pulled back the wrapping and then replaced it. "No swelling or redness. Definitely not poisonous."

"I didn't even see the snake," said Miri.

"Maybe we're just used to watching," said Felissa. "Soon you'll learn to notice movement that doesn't belong."

Miri doubted that. In a swamp, everything was moving all the time.

"I mean, *if* you stay," Felissa added. Though she said

it with a smile, her tone seemed to imply she was certain that Miri would not be staying.

A stubbornness coursed through Miri, hot as imagined venom. But she just asked, "Were you successful this morning?"

"Not bad." Astrid had a second rodent beside the rat in her belt, and Sus's basket held a couple of handfuls of tiny fish, some reed roots, and a green plant, still wet. Astrid tossed the rat at Miri's feet. "Think you can be useful?"

"Astrid, she's a city girl and a lady," Felissa said under her breath. Apparently despite Miri's disclosure about her mountain home, she had been so inept in the swamp they just could not believe she was anything but a pampered noble.

Miri picked up the rat, turned it over, grabbed a knife from a pot, and started to skin it. Really, it was not much different than skinning a rabbit.

On Mount Eskel, the villagers slaughtered their rabbits in high winter, when food was scarce and rabbit fur thickest. When Miri had been eight years old, she'd seen her sister, Marda, holding a rabbit over a stone, the knife in her hand trembling, her tears coming fast.

"Wait!" Miri had run out into the knee-deep snow. "I'll do it, Marda, I'll do it."

Miri had sweated over the task, her hands clumsy in the attempt to be swift. But new fur meant she could patch her old and useless winter cap into something that actually kept her ears warm. And for the first time, Marda did not cry when eating rabbit stew.

This rat was already dead, and Miri peeled off its skin even and quick. She cleaned it, pushed a wooden skewer through the body, and tidied up the limbs with pieces of green swamp grass so they wouldn't dangle.

Astrid's mouth hung open.

"Isn't it amazing," Miri said slyly, "what a person can learn from a book?"

Though the little house was mostly empty, it had a fine hearth with hooks for skewers and an iron pot. The water was already hot, and Sus added the small fish and chopped-up plant. They ate the soup, washed their clothes and the floor of the house, and by lunch hour the rodents were roasted and ready.

Miri watched King Fader's potential brides sit cross-legged on the floor, eating rat meat with their fingers, breaking off tiny ribs to pick it out of their teeth. These were the girls who could help Miri win Mount Eskel away from the king and merchants. These were the girls who might prevent a war.

Sus sucked the rat's roasted eyeballs out of its skull. Astrid burped.

Miri looked out the window toward Mount Eskel. No mountains in view. All she could see was land so wet it was indistinguishable from water. A flock of geese crossed the sky, their honks as brash and abrupt as an alarm of warning.

Chapter Five

The sun is staring, the water is fine
Little lily lie, lie a little low
The sweet river flow mixes into brine
Little lily lie, lie down below

Evening in the swamp rustled and stretched, clamoring for cooler hours. Other than the linder house at her back, Miri could see no other stone. Everything was alive and moving. The air teemed with birds, insects, and shadows of things flying. The grasses shook with the wind and with not-wind. The reeds whispered and clicked together, hiding creatures that scurried and jumped. The surface of the water trailed with the paths of skating bugs and arched with the movement of fish and larger animals. Everywhere was the sense of life just out of sight.

The girls sat outside after dinner near the water's edge. They were stuffing tiny seedpods into the ends of short, thick reeds and blowing, challenging one another to see who could shoot a seed the farthest over the water.

"Now would be a good time to start with your studies," Miri said.

"What studies?" asked Sus, cramming in more seeds. In the dimming light, her hair looked nearly black, the crinkly locks standing up around her head like the branches of a bramble bush.

"I think we should start with reading," said Miri, "and once you're comfortable, we can move on to other subjects, like History. You're going to love History!"

Astrid laughed. "When would we have time for studying?"

"Well, now?" said Miri, not meaning for it to be a question.

"We're just about to go check the traps and set them again for tomorrow's breakfast."

"You must have a way to purchase food or pay others to hunt it for you," said Miri.

"Pay with what exactly?" Astrid asked, eyes narrowed.

"With your allowance . . ." Miri did not need to look around again to realize that the king's money, supposedly sent each month from Asland, never made it to this little linder house.

"*Allowance*," Sus said slowly, her mouth trying out the unfamiliar word.

"If you just sit and read, then you won't eat," said Astrid.

"Unless you're Fat Hofer," said Sus.

Felissa nodded wisely. "Fat Hofer can do nothing and stay fat. I think he has magic."

"Magic isn't real," said Sus. "I think he eats flies."

Felissa dropped her reed. "He does not! I've never seen him eat a single fly."

"Then maybe he *absorbs* them," Sus said. She paused to blow. Her seeds flew, landing with light ripples on the dark water. "Flies land on his skin to suck his blood, but instead his skin sucks *them* in. They say he knows everything. I think he knows how to get fat on flies."

Felissa looked at Astrid and laughed.

"I want to absorb flies," Sus said in her serious manner.

"Never mind about Fat Hofer," Miri said. "Look, I have to teach you. The king said so."

"*Pbbt,*" said Astrid, blowing air through her lips. "Never met the king."

"I didn't want to attend a princess academy at first either," Miri said.

"A princess what?" Felissa asked.

"Academy. Like a school. Whenever a crown prince reaches the age of betrothal, the priests of the creator god divine which province or territory of Danland is home to his future bride. A graduate of a previous princess academy is chosen as tutor and sent to form a school there. It used to be just a formality and the highest ranking noble girls of the province attended for just a few days before the prince threw a ball and chose his bride. But in my case, none of us were noble. Or educated. Or considered fit bridal material for a royal highness. So we attended a real academy for over a year, and what I learned there changed everything for me and my village."

Astrid blinked slowly like a lizard sunning. "And what use would a princess academy have for us? We're not going to marry the crown prince."

Miri blanched. "Um . . . right. Of course not. The king, your cousin, just wants you to have the benefit of an education. If I can find a way to buy food so you don't have to hunt for it, will you do lessons with me each day? At least for a few hours?"

"Why not," Astrid said, as if she believed that would never happen.

The next morning when the girls went out to hunt, Miri stayed behind to do some sewing. She finished converting the yellow dress into a tunic shirt with leggings while the girls were still out, so she walked toward the village.

Miri's village on Mount Eskel was built from rocks stacked and secured together to make houses. But there were no rocks in the swamp. Though a wood grew nearby, those trees were all thin, wispy things with crooked branches. They must have been impractical for building houses because the Lesser Alvans only used reeds.

The houses had thick reed-bundle frames, wrapped and draped with woven mats. The roof mats were tightly woven to keep out the rain, while the wall mats were filled with holes to invite breezes. Most of the huts were barely large enough for a couple of people to lie down head to feet.

The ground of the village island appeared to be swampland covered by a strewn reed flooring. It was not until Miri was near the middle of the village and felt the ground shift beneath her that she understood she was not on land at all. The entire island was made of stacked reeds floating in the water. How thick would the false island have to be in order to float?

Miri spotted two smaller reed islands nearby. She could see the top layer of reeds was still green, then beneath that lay the golden white of dried reeds. The oldest reeds in the water were a dirty gray. The reeds on the bottom must decompose in the water. Miri saw a woman laying down fresh reeds around a house. Miri asked if she could direct her to Fat Hofer. The woman pointed but did not seem eager to engage in conversation with a stranger.

Miri knew she was on the main island of the village because it hosted the chapel. Fourteen pillars made of thick reed bundles stood straight, bending and meeting at the top to form a peaked roof. Woven mats formed the walls and roof.

Beside the chapel sat a man, his bald head protected with a cap, his legs covered with a cloth. He rested his hands on his belly, his lids half-closed as if he were about to nap.

"Fat Hofer?" Miri said. She had seen far fatter men in Asland, but he did look in good health, clearly not scrabbling to keep from starvation.

He squinted at her, lifting the brim of his cap against the sun. "I heard a lady of Asland had come to Lesser Alva. How good of you to attend me so soon after your arrival."

Miri squatted beside him. "You don't absorb flies."

"What?"

"You don't work yet you don't starve. Which means people pay you. For what? You sit here, seemingly doing nothing. But you're not doing nothing, are you? You're watching, you're learning, and then you trade information or advice for coins or food. You *know* things."

Fat Hofer laughed, his folded hands shaking on his

belly. "What an outrageous claim! I won't even take the time to deny it."

"The king's officials send the sisters an allowance every month. They should have enough for food and clothing at least. But they have nothing. Please tell me what happens to their coin."

He lowered his hat back over his eyes and put out his hand, palm up. "Nothing gets you nothing, my lady."

"I don't have any coin, but I do have a silk dress I can trade you," she said.

"What good is a silk dress here? Come talk to me when you have a coin or at least food to share."

Perhaps she could sell a dress to someone else.

She returned to the linder house and went through her bag, picking out a dress not too fancy but nice enough, and laid it over a windowsill so the humid air might work out the wrinkles. Miri used their outhouse and cleaned it, and then went for a short walk to hunt more of the water plants.

When she came back, the girls were home, and the silk dress was gone.

"Did one of you move the dress?" Miri asked.

"You mean the one you left out for anyone to come steal?" said Astrid. "Toad toots, girl, don't you know how to take care of your things?"

54

"None but a bandit would dare enter another's house," said Felissa. "But something hanging out a window? Anyone could steal that and no one would blame them. Always keep your things inside a house."

"Or in a boat," said Sus. "Though we don't have a boat."

"Um . . . my dress?" asked Miri.

"I hid your things for you," said Felissa. "Just in case someone saw the fancy dress and decided to risk some thievery."

The linder house had a cramped attic reached by climbing the wall and removing a flat stone. Miri followed Felissa up. Besides her dress, there were treasures that had belonged to their mother: a portrait of a woman, its paint streaking from heat; worm-eaten clothes; a glass-headed doll with a painted face; and stacks of letters.

Miri brought the letters down.

For supper they ate raw roots and stuck the tiny fish on sticks, roasting them over the fire till they were browned and crunchy.

"What happened to your parents?" Miri asked.

Sus and Felissa looked at their older sister. Astrid tested a fish with her fingers and then set it back over the embers to cook longer.

"Our ma died," Astrid said at last. "Several years ago. Her name was Elin. We never knew our father."

Sus reached out, placing her arm on Astrid's knee. Felissa leaned her head on Astrid's shoulder. Astrid put her arms around them both, a knot of sisters.

Miri had not seen her own sister in over a year. Separation felt like a fever—a wrongness and ache on her skin, as tangible as the lack of a touch.

With Astrid's permission, Miri read the letters. They were all formal, brief notes from a king's official in Asland, sent each month with the allowance. Starting about ten years before, the letters no longer came every month, sometimes missing several in a row. Around the time of Elin's death, the letters ceased altogether.

"We used to have coins to buy food from the traders," said Astrid, "but when Ma died, I couldn't find any coins and figured we'd run out. I never knew they'd been coming from the king."

Where was that money going now? Did it even leave Asland?

From the village Miri could hear singing. At first, just a single child's voice, high and piercing, too distant for her to unstring the words from the night. And then more voices. The song became as wild and loud as the swamp itself, and then it softened, became melancholy, a ballad or dirge perhaps. But even when the song was as quick and high as a dance, it always sounded lonely to Miri. Far away. Unwelcoming.

She could not see the water outside the window. She could not even hear a ripple over the honks and croaks, rasps and cries of the swamp. But she was aware of it, the breeze wet, the feeling of greatness and endlessness, like that of standing on a mountain's edge and sensing the cliff beyond. A cliff did not border emptiness. It met up with a great deal of air and falling. And falling was something, just as water was something.

Miri could sense the vastness of the ocean out there, and she felt displaced, a flower uprooted, tossed onto the water, pulled into the current.

Chapter Six

Trader, trader
Bone and stone
Pay it later
Get a loan

From the cracking and cawing moment of dawn, Miri was waiting where the forest path from Greater Alva spilled into the swamp. Over a week in Lesser Alva and at last a trading day had come. And not the sporadic traders who came from Greater Alva but the monthly merchants who traveled all the way from Asland. Those traders would carry letters.

She heard the creak of cart wheels and the snorts of donkeys before she spied the first trader trudge through the trees. A dozen more followed him. She ran forward.

"I am Miri Larendaughter, lady of the princess and envoy of King Bjorn to Lesser Alva. I am here to claim anything that has come from the king or his officials for his royal cousins in the linder house."

The first trader tipped up his large-brimmed hat and smiled. His expression seemed as sincere as a snake's. He wore muddied boots high as his knees, but his shirt was silk and his cap fine wool. "I'm Gunnar, head trader, and I'm obliged to check in with Jeffers first, my lady fanciness, and then I'll come *straight* to you."

"I'll join you."

Gunnar's smile twitched. "As you wish, my lady."

Most of the trading goods were stacked in small, two-wheeled wagons pulled by donkeys. The traders unhitched the donkeys on shore and pulled the carts themselves onto the main reed island.

The water was crowded with reed boats, people journeying from other islands all over Lesser Alva for trading day. Nearly hidden by the crowd, Miri spotted Fat Hofer still beside the chapel, his cap shading his watching eyes.

Gunnar approached a large reed house near the chapel and clapped his hands, since there was a woven reed curtain instead of a wood door to knock on. The door lifted to a man dressed in a blue linen shirt and fine trousers, his face browned, his beard cut to a point on his chin. Such beards had started going out of fashion in Asland years ago, and Miri had not seen anyone else keeping the style other than the chief delegate.

"Good morning, Jeffers," said Gunnar.

"Good morning, all," Jeffers said. "Welcome! You may enter my house."

Gunnar and two other traders pushed in past Miri. She introduced herself and moved to enter too, but Jeffers blocked her way.

"I would invite you in, but we have business," Jeffers said and let the door flap shut.

Miri waited. She paced. The top of her head began to burn in the sun. Jeffers's house rumbled with laughter. She clenched her fists, but instead of punching through the door flap, she politely clapped.

Jeffers opened the curtain. His house was one large room. The woven reed walls and thick pillars were a bright gold, but the ceiling, darkened by smoke, was the color of oiled wood. Miri was surprised to see furniture like a real wood table, several chairs, and a reed mattress atop a wooden bed frame. Several men lay sleeping on mats.

"I believe there is a letter from Asland for the girls in the linder house," Miri said.

Jeffers took the mailbag from Gunnar and went through the few folded and sealed papers.

"No, nothing," Jeffers said. He smiled at Miri. "Sorry I couldn't be of service. I'd invite you in, but I'm afraid my establishment isn't hospitable to a fine lady such as yourself."

Behind him, one of the sleeping men roused, rubbed his head, and stared at Miri.

"Very well," she whispered.

As the door flap shut, the laughter renewed.

She stalked back to Fat Hofer and asked, "Who is Jeffers?"

He held out his palm.

"I'm warning you," she said, "I'm in a mood to put someone on a spit and—"

He put both his hands up in defense. "I'm just trying to stay alive, since I sadly cannot absorb flies."

"I promise I'll pay you when I can," Miri said. "Which will be sooner with your help. Please."

Fat Hofer stared at her, rubbed his large nose, and sniffed. "All right then. Jeffers is the closest thing we have to a head of the village. He negotiates with the traders and sets the prices for all of Lesser Alva. His house is the largest and every night fills up with villagers who want to play darts and buy swill."

"Swill?" Miri asked.

"A clear, scorching drink he makes himself," he said. "Makes him pretty popular."

"Not with me. He's bribing the traders to let him steal the mail and the girls' allowance. I'm so livid I could eat a snake."

61

"You should know something," Fat Hofer said.

Miri leaned forward, her breath held.

"Snakes," he said, "are delicious."

Miri scowled. "I have to go back to Asland and tell them what's happening here."

"Planning to walk to Greater Alva yourself? Bandits called those woods home not so long ago and perhaps still do. If you do get to the port, how will you pay passage to board a ship?"

Miri stared at her bare feet, dried mud cracking off her toes. She felt as squashed as a toad in a wheel rut.

"If you find someone who will buy a silk dress, I'll give you ten percent of what I make."

"That's thinking like a Lesser Alvan!" he said. "But alas, Lady Miri, no one in Lesser Alva cares about a silk dress. And unless you have solid coin, the traders arrange trades only through Jeffers. After your display, I'd guess Jeffers won't be willing to do any business with you."

But she had to try. She was here to teach the girls, and she could not do that if they were busy as birds hunting for food every hour of the day. So Miri fetched one of Britta's dresses and returned to Jeffers's house.

She clapped timidly and peered through the door curtain.

More of the traders had joined the others in the house,

sitting cross-legged on mats, eating flat bread, chatting in small groups.

Jeffers leaned back in one of the wooden chairs, made cozy with frayed pillows. He smiled, but his eyes were unwelcoming.

"Yes?" he said.

"I have a dress I'd like to sell," she said quietly.

Jeffers took a slow drink from a clay-fired mug. "It's not proper for a lady to sell her own clothing off her back, now is it? Allow me to save your reputation by declining. But in good news, I found letters addressed to you!"

He handed them to a young boy who brought them to the door.

"Apologies, the wax seals must have cracked on the journey," Jeffers said with a shameless smile.

She recognized the handwriting on the letters: one from Peder and one from Marda. She fingered the first letter's broken wax and almost spoke an accusation when she noticed a blocky man with long hair and a bushy beard in the back of the house. A scar ran through one eye and split his cheek. Miri's feet and hands felt icy cold.

I know him. How do I know him?

His meaty, scarred hand held onto the hilt of the curved dagger in his belt. He started to turn, as if he would look to see who Jeffers was talking to.

Miri let the door close. She turned and ran from Jeffers's house and off the island, her heartbeats keeping pace with her feet.

Dogface. That was what he was called. Two years ago she'd watched him and his fellow bandits depart Mount Eskel in a snowstorm. What would he do if he recognized the girl who spoiled their raid and led their chief over a cliff?

Bandits have no honor. Bandits love only coin and death.

Back at the house, Miri fetched ink, quill, and parchment from her bag and wrote a hasty letter to Britta, reporting what was happening with Jeffers and the allowance.

When she returned to town the traders were gone. She kept running, her side aching, and caught them a few minutes into the woods.

"Here!" she called. "Here's a letter, if you please. For Princess Britta at the white stone palace. She'll pay you for its delivery."

A young trader took it but looked at Gunnar with an eyebrow raised.

"Give it here," said Gunnar. "I'll take care of it, my lady."

"Um, perhaps it would be best if I went with you and carried the letter myself," she said.

"You could join us," said Gunnar. "Unfortunately I couldn't *guarantee* your safety, not being king-sworn myself."

Another trader was standing very close beside her. She could feel his hot exhales on the top of her head.

"No, th-thank you," she said. "Just . . . please, deliver the letter. The princess will pay you well."

Miri hurried away, not stopping until she reached the shade of the linder house to read the letters.

Dear Miri,

I am writing from our camp a day's ride from Asland, and the messenger just gave me your letter. I will send this note back with him. I will let your father and sister know you are not coming and give them your things.

I want to say something cheery so you will not feel sad. But I cannot think of a thing. I guess I do not have your imagination. Perhaps we never should have gone to Asland. Perhaps it is a safer life when a king and queen do not know your name.

I know you want me to return to Mount Eskel and my father, so I will. Spring seems so far away.

Thank you for working to win Mount Eskel's land for us. But I am angry that you have to, so angry I just crushed a beetle beneath my boot. I am trying to impress

*you with how strong and manly I am. Let all the beetles in
Asland fear me and my terrifying boots!*

Thank you all the same.

*Be careful. A swamp sounds like a thing one could fall
into and never be seen again. And I would very much like
to see you again.*

> *Yours,*
> *Peder*

Miri lifted the paper to her nose, but all she could
smell was dust and wind, no lingering tang of ink, no
warmth of Peder's hands. Her heart seemed to curl up
like a snail disappearing into its shell.

She unfolded the next letter, careful not to rip the
paper.

For Miri my sister,

*I have read the letters you sent us from Asland so
many times I should know how to write one myself. Please
tell me if I am doing it wrong. I just talk to you in words
on a page, right? I feel silly talking when you are not here
to answer.*

*Peder told us you are not coming home yet. I know you
must want to. You are probably worried that we are sad.
Please do not worry about us. But please come home soon.*

Pa is well. He misses you. In the quarry I am doing squaring as well as stone braking. The autumn weather is mild. We have enough food.

Please come home.

Marda

Miri reread the letters for the rest of the day. In the warm, sticky night she lay awake remembering again and again the moment when she'd said good-bye to Peder in the palace courtyard. Why hadn't she stayed longer? Kissed him again? Held him so tight she might be holding him still? Instead she lay alone on a hard reed mat accosted by a night sharp with croaks and clicks, so far away from home she could not remember the scent of the high mountains, the sound of Marda's voice, or the exact color of Peder's eyes.

Chapter Seven

⮞⮜⮞⮜⮞

Gray for sparrow, red for ant
Green for the sapling of the deep water plant
Black for spider, orange for moth
Brown for the coverings cut from cloth

That night, Miri went to sleep aching for home. But instead of dreams of Marda, Peder, and Pa, Miri's mind danced with visions of people she had never seen before.

Twin girls with bright red hair. She saw them against the backdrop of stone in the linder house like a watercolor painting on parchment. Three women sat on chairs, talking while the little girls played with painted wood animals. Outside the window, a cluster of reed houses.

In the morning, the dream still clung to Miri, invisible yet tangible, like a spiderweb caught on her arms.

Though the door was open and the windows just empty stone frames, the house felt closed up and airless. Miri went to the outhouse, and heat and wet air followed her like a swarm of gnats. Sometimes she swatted at a tickle on her forehead or the backs of her knees only to discover there was no snake or biting insect—just dripping sweat.

The sisters spent that day the same as the last—fishing, hunting, trapping, and cleaning. Even though they passed all their time gathering food, at night Miri's stomach felt like half of itself. She'd gotten used to three full meals each day at the palace in Asland. She was not the same tough mountain girl she'd once been.

When Miri tried to talk to the girls about Arithmetic, Etiquette, and other subjects, Astrid hushed her.

"We're not your students, and you're not our pooter-tutor."

Felissa giggled.

The girls let Miri tell stories at least. While standing in knee-deep water, trying to net fish, Miri recounted the history of Queen Gertrud.

Miri had first heard the account while studying at the Queen's Castle. Hundreds of years ago, King Jorgan had bought linder blocks from Mount Eskel, hauled them to Asland, and built a white stone palace. And when the minister of defense had tried to turn the old red-brick castle on the river island into a prison, King Jorgan's wife, Queen Gertrud, claimed it instead to use for education. It became known as the Queen's Castle and served as a university.

"My friends and I told Gertrud's story to Queen Sabet, Danland's current queen. I think it gave her courage to help us when we needed her. Until then, I don't think she really believed a queen could do much of anything."

"What is Queen Sabet like?" asked Felissa.

"She's timid. No," Miri said, realizing, "she's sad. She must have been remarkable when she was at her princess academy for the king to choose her from the others."

"Does she have anyone to hug her?" Felissa asked.

Miri blinked at the oddness of the question.

"She's a queen," Astrid said, waving her hand. "She probably has servants paid just to give her hugs."

Felissa laughed at the idea. "Still, I don't like to think of someone sad and alone in a big house."

A wriggle of movement caught Miri's eye. She screamed and scrambled ashore.

"It's only my net!" said Astrid. "Soggy bottom bellows, Miri, but you just woke up the world."

"Give yourself more time, you'll get used to noticing unusual movement," Felissa said.

Miri had barely recovered from the frightening sight of Astrid's net-that-was-not-a-snake when a pop cracked the air. Miri dropped to a crouch.

"What are you doing?" Astrid asked.

"A musket fired!" said Miri. "Hide in the reeds, maybe the war has begun."

"What war?"

"That was probably just a burst berry," said Felissa.

She led Miri to a nearby bush. Hanging heavy among the greenish blue leaves were perfectly round berries. Felissa picked two. One was white and small. The other was twice its size and looked painfully bloated, the skin stretched and nearly transparent. Inside, Miri could see lots of black seeds.

"The berries keep growing bigger and bigger till they burst," said Felissa.

She clapped the large berry between her palms. Again that sharp popping sound, and the seeds flew out in all directions. Miri flinched. Poisonous snakes were silent, harmless berries were loud, and in the middle of it all, Miri could not tell what was dangerous.

When four weeks had inched by and at last the Aslandian traders returned to Lesser Alva, Miri was waiting at the mouth of the road. Surely Britta and Steffan would have sent a wagonload of supplies or a wallet of gold coins.

There was nothing.

And from Jeffers: "No letter for you or the stone house sisters, my lady."

Miri sat on the reeds beside Fat Hofer. She rested her face in her hands, her elbows on her knees.

"What happened?" she asked, her words smooshed like her cheeks between her hands. "I told the traders Britta would pay them for delivering my letter."

"Come now, my lady, surely you've guessed that Jeffers would pay them more not to." Fat Hofer scratched his bald head beneath his cap. "Write innocent love letters, they won't interfere. They're likely eager for those letters to go through and assure everyone in the capital that you're well, giving no reason to send anyone here to investigate. But a letter that alerts the capital to possibly shady dealings in Lesser Alva will mysteriously disappear—what am I saying?"

He pulled his hat back down over his eyes and shut his mouth.

"I won't tell that you talk to me for free," Miri said.

"*Not* for free," he said. "You will pay me back one day."

Miri returned to the house and wrote a letter to Britta that made no mention of Jeffers or the king's allowance. Instead she told a tale of girls kept prisoner by a mean uncle and denied food. But she named one of the girls Flower, hoping Britta would understand. Miri was named for a flower that grew on the slopes of Mount Eskel.

Miri sent the letter with the traders, but even if Britta did understand her message, Miri suspected it would be in vain. She'd let Jeffers and the traders know her intentions. Any letter of hers to the palace was bound to fall overboard on the journey back to Asland.

When Miri returned to the linder house, the sisters were just back from hunting. Miri brought out one of her books.

"It's time to study," she called out.

Astrid did not look up from the fish she was deboning. "There's nothing you have in those books that will be a seedpod of help to us here, so quit trying."

"I haven't been able to get your allowance for you yet," Miri said, keeping her voice calm. "But we can't wait any longer. The king sent me here to educate you. The first step is learning to read."

"She's mad," Sus said, her blue-eyed stare so intense Miri flinched.

"Mmhm," said Felissa. "Crackling mad."

"Like fat in the fire," said Astrid, nodding.

"What? I am not. I . . . I . . . ." Miri noticed her fists were clenched. She forced them to relax. "I'm just—"

"Mad," said Sus.

Miri rubbed her face and cursed herself. She could pretend all she wanted, but these girls would know the truth. And she'd just realized why. *Linder-wisdom*. Well, at least she could teach them *something* they might want to know.

"Felissa, how do you think Sus is feeling right now?"

Felissa squinted at her sister. "Mm, smug."

"How do you know that?"

"Well, she *looks* smug."

"Let's play a game." Miri blindfolded Felissa and made a quiet gesture to the other girls. Silently, she strutted in a crouch, flapping her elbows as if she were a chicken. Astrid gaped. Sus covered her mouth with her hands, her eyes smiling.

"Now how is Sus feeling?" Miri asked.

"Um, she's happy. Or something," said Felissa.

"And Astrid?"

"She's kind of annoyed I think. What are you all doing?" Felissa took off her blindfold.

"Chicken," Sus said, pointing at Miri.

Miri pointed back. "Linder-wisdom. That's how you know. I can't sense what you're feeling. I haven't lived inside linder for long enough. But you three can. The royal family in Asland has spent most of their lives inside the linder wings of the palace and they have this same talent. Emotions bounce back from linder, and you've gained the ability to sense that echo when you're inside this house."

"Yes! That's true, about outside and inside!" Felissa clapped her hands as if Miri had performed a trick.

"I'd never thought about it before," said Sus, "but it sounds true."

"Something you didn't know, Astrid," said Miri. "Something I was able to teach you."

Astrid shrugged. "All you did was put a fancy name to what we can already do."

Miri opened her mouth to answer but had nothing to say.

Astrid passed very close to Miri on her way outside and whispered, "And I'm older than you, *tutor.*"

Miri stood alone there for some time, listening to the girls' talk mix with the chirps of swamp sparrows, rude quacks of ducks, and singing from the village islands. A thousand conversations just out of reach.

She pressed her foot against the linder floor and called out in quarry-speech. The memory she silently sang was of the night she'd spent trapped in a closet at the princess academy, forgotten and alone. Everyone who would be able to detect her quarry-speech was much too far away, but she kept on anyway.

Written Autumn Week Ten
Never received

Dear Peder,

I do not know why you think well of me. I seem to remember a time when I was passably useful. On Mount Eskel I could milk the goats and make cheese. How I would love to make cheese right now! Instead of sweating in a swamp not catching fish. Or lizards or rats or turtles or ducks.

And definitely not teaching three girls how to be princesses.

I would run home to you if I could. Even knowing what it would mean to our village to own the land under us, I would abandon my duty if I had any hope of making it home. Now you surely cannot be thinking well of me.

Thinking well of you at least,

Miri

The Forgotten Sisters

Written Autumn Week Ten
Never received

For Miri my sister,

I hoped to get a letter from you before winter closed the pass, but the first snows have come. No chance in sending this to you now before spring. I will write anyway. It is nice to pretend you can hear me.

Last week, Peder and his father were arguing. The entire village could hear. Peder wanted to go back for you. His pa said Peder's place is on Mount Eskel. Time to return to quarry work and forget Asland. And forget you too, since you were too enchanted with the lowlands to return home.

Peder ran out of the house. I joined him later on that huge, chair-shaped boulder that looks out over the cliff. He asked me if you would come home if you could, and I said yes.

I brought out the stack of letters you had written to me from Asland over the past year. He read them all. Sometimes he frowned, but mostly he smiled.

He said he was going to find you. I said of course. And so he packed up clothes and food in a blanket and left.

Surely he will find you before spring, when the traders might come to take you this letter. For now, it will sit lonely here on the mantel.

Your sister,
Marda

Chapter Eight

⁂

The water slips, the water blinks
The water tips its tail
The water dips, the water sinks
The water shows its scales
What water unhinges its jaws?
The most dangerous kind that was

Miri was so tired of being damp. Her body itched with constant sweat. Her clothes got wet in the morning from splashing through water on the hunt and never really dried. Her feet were filthy, her hair was sticky and frizzed out around her face, pestering her forehead and cheeks with every breeze. She felt more like a scuttling rodent than a person.

And she was tired. So many dreams. The redheaded twins, doing nothing, just playing, sitting, sleeping. She was annoyed with herself for not having more interesting dreams.

Last night in addition to the twins, she had dreams

of Astrid and Felissa. They'd been younger, but she'd still known it was them in that way that dreams worked.

"Who lived here before you?" Miri asked, sloshing through hip-deep water with a net.

"Nobody," said Astrid.

"But the house is old." *And full of memories*, Miri thought and wondered if it were true. Could a house's memories infiltrate her dreams? "Did your mother say how she came to live here?"

"She said it was the best place for us," said Felissa. "That it was safe."

Miri slapped a fat mosquito feasting on her arm. She looked back toward the house and considered returning to write to Peder again, even if the letter would never get farther than Jeffers's hands. Maybe she'd just keep writing to him and Marda and Britta until this boulder in her chest rolled out and let her heart beat freely again.

"Don't move!" Astrid called out suddenly.

Miri froze. Another snake? She did not want to hold still. She wanted to scream and flail and claw her way out of the water and far from Lesser Alva. But if Astrid said not to move, then she was not in danger of a mere toothless worm.

Astrid was in the water off to her side. She had her knife out.

"I'm going to get it," Astrid whispered.

"Miri, move slowly to shore," Sus whispered. *"Slowly.* Astrid, a little to your left. Felissa . . ."

Sus handed one pole to Felissa and backed away, taking up a position on shore so the three sisters formed a triangle.

Miri slowly backed up, scanning for a snake. All she noticed was a log floating in the thick green water. Coming closer. And the log had eyes.

Miri could no longer get her legs to move. She could not even manage to breathe.

Sus's and Felissa's poles dangled loops of rope at one end. Miri had seen the girls use them to hook fowl by the neck. Felissa widened the loop. Astrid was coming closer, her eyes never leaving the not-log.

"Ready?" Astrid asked.

"Go for the neck," Sus whispered. "Remember last time. Aim true."

"Strike swiftly," said Felissa.

There was no warning. The beast lunged for Miri, its impossibly huge mouth open and full of long, crooked teeth. Miri screamed and scrambled back. The beast's mouth snapped shut, just a hand's breadth from Miri's foot. And it would have gotten her too, if Felissa had not hooked its head and pulled up on the pole. Sus's pole had missed. She kept trying to hook the beast from the other side.

The beast lunged again, but Astrid sprang onto its back, driving her knife into its soft, white throat. The beast thrashed, long, thick tail whipping. Sus managed to loop its neck just before both Astrid and the animal went underwater. The pole began to slip from Sus's hands. Miri crawled up beside Sus, grabbed on, and helped pull.

They yanked its head out of the water. It had twisted and was upside down, thrashing, blood oozing from its neck and making blackish clouds in the green water.

"Astrid!" Miri shouted.

A hand seized the beast from the water. Another followed, still gripping a knife. Astrid pulled herself on top of the beast and stabbed again. This time the thrashing slowed.

Astrid clambered up the bank, threw aside her knife, and took hold of Felissa's pole.

"Pull!" Astrid said. "Pull!"

And with each call, the girls pulled, inching the beast out of the water.

It had stopped moving. The girls all fell to the ground, muddy and exhausted. The animal lay between them, longer than Miri and Sus put together, its eyes cloudy like a struck fish's. It had dark-green, hard, and knobby skin and four short legs with long claws. Beside its narrow, teeth-filled head and long tail, its stout body seemed tiny.

Miri stared at teeth the length of her thumb and shivered in the muggy sunlight. She felt Sus shiver beside her. Astrid was breathing hard.

Felissa giggled. She looked at Astrid, waggling her eyebrows, and smiled hugely. Astrid giggled too.

And then all three girls began to laugh. Miri gazed at them. Had they lost their minds? They'd almost been killed! Felissa put her arms around her sisters' shoulders, reaching out to put a hand on Miri's back.

"It's not every day something tries to eat you, huh, Miri?" said Felissa, laughing.

Miri smiled. The relief and the smile mixed together in her, making her stomach ticklish till she laughed too.

"That was a big one," Astrid whispered.

"Really big," said Felissa. "Bigger than the one the villagers brought in last month."

"We brought in one too, last year," said Sus.

"Yes, but they all said it was small and skinny and anybody could've done it," said Astrid, "and that it takes a man to bag a big caiman."

"This will show them," said Felissa.

"Woo-wee!" Astrid shouted. "That's a lot of meat."

"You're bleeding," Miri said, gesturing to Astrid's cheek.

Astrid touched her face and then examined the scratches on her hands.

"Not as badly as the caiman did. I win." She smiled wide.

It took an hour to drag the caiman back to the linder house.

"Good work, Miri," Astrid said, huffing with the effort. "Your clumsy movements attracted this beast. We should use you as bait more often."

"She's kidding," Felissa said, equally out of breath.

Miri nodded. She could not find the air to respond.

When they finally reached home, Astrid scaled the house and stood on the roof. Cupping her hands around her mouth, she shouted toward the village, "We've got meat! We've got meat!"

There was a small answering shout, then another. She made her announcement again, and more voices responded, repeating her words.

A man came running up the slope to the linder house. Miri recognized him as one she'd seen at Jeffers's house. He was holding a knife with a serrated edge.

Miri ducked behind the house and hissed at Astrid. "What are you doing? He's going to steal your caiman!"

Astrid rolled her eyes.

"This much meat would rot before we could eat it all," said Sus, "so if you bag a caiman, you share a caiman. It's sacred law."

"Big one," said the man approvingly. "That'll feed forty."

"Forty!" Astrid called from the roof. "Meat for forty!"

"One caiman alone can't feed all the villagers," Felissa explained to Miri. "So for this feast, only the first forty get a piece."

The movement from the islands reminded Miri of a hive of ants fleeing a flooded nest. Everyone, it seemed, wanted to take part in the feast. People ran up the hill, offering dried peat for a fire, baskets of water plants, or stacks of flat brown bread. Two other men squatted by the first to help butcher the caiman, expertly cutting up pieces of meat and placing them on a reed mat. A stooped woman put some of the guts into a pot. Another man scraped the fat off the skin and sprinkled it with salt to dry it out. Such a skin would be worth something to traders. Miri suspected that if a person did not contribute to the meal in some way, they were not invited to stay. There would be others ready to take their place. Astrid stood over it all, queen of the feast, her arms folded, smiling.

Miri stayed inside at first, keeping an eye out for that bandit Dogface. Cook fires sputtering in mud holes, with pots of water heating for the stew of organ meat and water plants. The villagers began threading chunks of white caiman meat onto green reeds and roasting them over the flames.

The smells of cooking meat made Miri's stomach plead. She took up a branch and chose a fireside, facing town to keep watch for Dogface.

She blew on a chunk of white meat and popped it in her mouth. The meat was denser than fish, chewy with a mildly spicy aftertaste. The image of the caiman attacking burst into her mind, and she squeezed her eyes shut. She took a deep breath and bit down on another piece of meat, chewing hard enough to kill. She was the predator now, she was the beast with teeth to fear, tearing and biting and killing!

"What are you smiling about?" Felissa asked, sitting beside her.

"Oh nothing," Miri said, blushing. "Well, just about how that caiman almost killed me. But now I'm chewing it up. And even though it's already dead—"

"It's still kind of satisfying?" Felissa asked.

"Prey becomes the predator," Miri said. "You know, maybe it is time I became a bandit."

Felissa laughed. "A bandit? You're too nice."

"I don't want to be too nice. I want to be as mean as they are."

"Or just more clever," said Sus, joining them.

"What are you talking about?" asked Astrid. Her mouth was full of meat, and around her neck hung a necklace of caiman teeth, punctured and threaded with a thin reed fiber. A gift, perhaps, made by someone who did not have anything else to share.

"Bandits," said Felissa.

"Naturally," said Astrid.

"Is it always wrong to steal?" said Miri. "Or at least, is it wrong to steal back what someone else stole from you?"

"Ask one of your books," said Astrid.

"If it's yours to begin with, then it's not stealing at all," said Sus, her chin in her hand as she watched the flames.

"What do you want to steal?" Felissa scooted closer, her smile huge.

"Your allowance," said Miri. "They preyed on us. Why can't we take a turn?"

At a far fire, Miri spotted him. Thick, bearded, scarred, eyes that seemed disinterested but never stopped looking. Dogface the bandit. Miri hurried inside.

The feast continued all day. Meat roasted over flame till the organ stew was ready, followed by thin slices of white belly skin crackling and crisping over the embers.

Miri watched it all through the window while making plans. Dogface had been a bandit once, and perhaps was one still. Certainly Jeffers and the trader Gunnar, despite their pretended respectability, were no better than common bandits.

Something had to change. Perhaps before the girls could learn to be princesses, Miri needed to teach them how to be bandits.

Chapter Nine

That caiman struck with yellow eyes flashing
Its eyes were as hot as the boiling sea
That caiman struck with yellow teeth gnashing
Each tooth was as long as a cypress tree

After two months in the swamp, the soles of Miri's feet were as tough as lizard skin, but the walk to the woods still poked and scuffed her. Here, the ground was drier and harder, and broken brambles bit like snakes. But the sisters did not complain, so neither did Miri.

She took them to the mouth of the narrow road that led to Greater Alva.

"Fat Hofer said bandits plagued these woods in the past," said Miri. "The king's guard recently broke up most bandit groups. But still, because of past attacks, the traders might assume any attackers are bandits. Certainly they wouldn't suspect royal cousins."

"That won't stop them from trying to kill us," said Astrid. "I don't care about stealing our allowance from them. We're doing fine without it."

"But that allowance is ours," said Felissa. "It was Ma's too. How can we just let them take it?"

"I want to try," said Sus.

"Once we get your money back we can buy food," said Miri. "Food like eggs and ground wheat and honey. I make the most amazing honey cakes!"

Astrid had no answer to that.

Miri felt reckless. The loneliness and weeks of inactivity bit her, a death grip threatening to pull her under. At last, a task! Something she could do to try to fulfill her duty.

"It'll be like bagging a caiman," said Miri. "Only this meat won't spoil. One big catch that's worth an entire month of hunts and traps."

Astrid looked thoughtfully into the forest canopy. Miri wagered that Astrid quite enjoyed hunting caiman.

"According to your mother's letters, the king's allowance used to come monthly with the traders from Asland," said Miri. "That's when we need to pounce. They might be prepared to squash a real bandit attack, but we're not trying to steal their goods. We just need to get in and out fast enough to slip away with one parcel."

"And how will we do that?" asked Astrid.

"We'll need a plan, Sus," said Miri.

"Me?" said Sus, her serious expression opened in surprise.

"Why Sus?" Astrid asked Miri.

"When the caiman attacked, Sus was the one telling us the plan," said Miri. "She's got a mind for strategy. You were the leader and chief actor. Felissa was the support and conflict resolver."

"Caimans are one thing," Sus said. "I don't know anything about bandits."

"Everything connects," said Miri. "Gunpowder was discovered first by circus performers and later adapted for muskets. Engineers learned skills from musket makers that improved things like bridges and locks. The more we know about everything, the easier we can make connections between one subject and another. What you know of caiman hunting might make you good bandits."

And maybe, she thought, *good bandits can become good princesses.*

"Sus is the planner, Felissa the support, and I'm the leader," said Astrid. "So what are you?"

"Me?" said Miri. "I'm your tutor."

They walked the forest path, scoping out the best ambush spots. Miri offered a general idea of what they could do.

"A diversion, and then someone swoops in fast to free the mail bag."

"I could do it. I'm fast," said Sus.

"You are not," said Astrid.

"I'm like the striking snake," Sus said, her face deadly earnest. "I'm a diving kestrel."

"I'm faster than you, froglet," said Astrid. "And I'm the oldest. If anyone's going to risk her neck, it'll be me."

The sisters debated this point the whole way back home. Miri kept silent. The more Astrid argued in favor of her banditry talents, the more she committed to the scheme. Miri yearned to chew up Jeffers and those traders so badly her jaw ached.

At the house, Miri stood at the threshold till one of them officially invited her in. It was Sus this time.

"I . . . uh . . . I'll need to teach you to read, just a little," said Miri. "If anything goes wrong with the plan, all of us should be prepared to get to the mail and read what's written on the envelopes."

Astrid raised one eyebrow. "Is this whole bandit thing just a trick to get us to read?"

Beginning that very day, Sus began spending as many hours with Miri as hunting allowed, learning the letters and the sounds they made. Sometimes Astrid and Felissa sat by too. While out hunting, they practiced writing their names in mud with a stick. They memorized the letters of one another's names, and of their mother's and Miri's. If the traders did have a letter from the palace, there was no telling whose name it would bear.

"Why do you care so much about teaching us to read anyway?" Astrid asked.

"Three years ago I didn't know how," said Miri. "But once I did, I learned things that made life on our mountain a lot better. Reading a book is like going on a great journey. You don't know what'll happen, but something is bound to change. And for me, that change has always been good."

Miri managed to sneak in other lessons besides reading. She told them about great historical battles under the pretense that the knowledge could help with strategy. She instructed them on Aslandian culture and social structure, because, she said, "Understanding how city folk like the traders think can only help."

The morning of trading day, they ate the rest of last night's supper, which had been simmering over the fire. It tasted like smoke and mud. Astrid filled their precious waterskin from the rain barrel and gave it to Felissa, who went ahead to watch from deep in the woods where the road was straightest.

The traders likely would not leave Greater Alva till after breakfast, and their journey would take half the day. But the girls were too anxious for hunting or other chores. They waited in the woods near the mouth of the road for word from Felissa.

The sun was angled toward afternoon when Felissa came running.

"There are more," said Felissa, out of breath. "There are a dozen more than last time."

"Our plan won't work," said Sus.

"That's it," said Astrid. "We've got to get out of here."

"Wait," said Sus. "If we had a bigger distraction, like in the Battle of Holgoth . . . Miri, you said that in Aslandian culture, men are supposed to behave a certain way around ladies. If Miri gets dressed all ladylike in one of her fancy dresses, she can be our distraction. All right, Astrid?"

Astrid frowned, but she nodded.

"You three carry on as you would," said Miri. "Remember, if you get caught, proclaim your name loudly. They'll kill some bandit quick but they'll hesitate to slay the king's cousin."

"Strike swiftly," said Felissa, repeating advice Miri had heard them give one another often while hunting.

"Aim true," said Sus.

Astrid said, "Let's go hunting."

Miri ran back to the house and dressed in Britta's finest silk gown. She put her hair up and stuck a feather in it. It was a heron feather, not a fancy dyed ostrich feather, but she gambled that the traders were not well versed in fashion. She washed her face and scraped dirt from under her fingernails. She hitched up her skirt to keep it out of the mud as she trudged up toward the woods, moving as slowly as she dared so that she would not sweat noticeably on the silk.

Miri was just a few minutes into the woods when she heard hooves on the narrow road. She did rush now. She had to get to the designated spot before the traders did.

She spotted Gunnar first, backed by the usual troop of traders, but he was also joined by armed men. There was no palace insignia on their armor, so they were not royal guards. The traders must have hired warriors for added protection on the road, which meant the roads had become more dangerous lately. That would certainly lend more credence to the girls' banditry charade. Then again, it could also earn them a sword point.

Miri stopped. She'd made a terrible mistake.

Those swords at their sides were sharp. The arrows in their quivers were tipped with steel. This was not a philosophical exercise Master Filippus was posing to students in the safety of the Queen's Castle. This was not a story in a book of tales. Miri was asking the girls to face real men with real muskets who could do real damage.

"Uh . . . ," she said cleverly.

Her mind was whirling, and there did not seem to be enough air to think. How could she warn the girls to stop without the traders catching on to what they had planned?

Astrid would not back off, not now, no matter what Miri did. Miri took a deep breath. *Don't hesitate*, she told herself. *Just swing.*

"Good day!" she said brightly. Her palms were sweating. She did not dare wipe them on the silk dress.

Gunnar groaned. "Come to accost us again before we've even arrived?"

"If that's what it takes to get what's rightfully mine."

"I told you, all the mail goes to Jeffers. You'll have to deal with him."

"Jeffers is stealing my mail," said Miri. "If it has my name on it, give it straight to me."

"And how am I supposed to know your name, eh? You could be any old swamp rat."

"Sir!" said one of the guards. "Don't speak so to a lady."

Guards coming to her defense. That was good.

"May I just look at the letters so I know if there is one for me?" asked Miri. "Then I'll wait for Jeffers to give it to me himself."

"The king's mail official trusts me to keep these safe,"

Gunnar said, patting the bag strapped to his donkey. "I won't let—"

A sawed-off treetop dropped onto the road. Miri jumped back and screamed. At that same moment, another treetop blocked the rear escape.

"What the—" Gunnar started.

Loud pops filled the air, and what seemed to be buckshot went flying into the group. Guards hollered and ducked, some running for cover as they were struck on their face and hands.

It was not musket fire, however—just Felissa and Sus blowing seeds through reed shooters while Astrid hammered burst berries between rocks. In the momentary chaos, Miri pulled out a small knife strapped to her ankle, cut the leather mailbag off Gunnar's donkey, and threw it into the brush beside the road. She could not risk going through the bag herself.

The noises stopped, and the men realized they had not actually been shot. Some of the guards fired muskets blindly into the woods. Miri shut her eyes, praying the girls had remembered to lie flat on the ground.

Some checked the animals for wounds and others searched the brush and trees beside the road, the guards with their swords out. Gunnar found the mailbag on the ground. He opened it to make sure the letters were still inside. Miri hoped that at least one was missing.

Miri looked around, all innocence, her hands clasped to her chest.

"My goodness, what *was* that?"

"Bandits," said a guard. "Their weapons must have misfired, lucky for us. We should pursue—"

"Oh oh," Miri said quickly. "I feel so . . ." She let her eyes roll up and fainted elegantly onto a bush. Moments later she felt herself being lifted into a wagon. She fluttered open her eyes and watched the guards clear the sawed-off tree from the road, declaring they should deliver the lady and the traders safely into town.

They were not pursuing the bandits. Miri felt so relieved she began to cry behind closed eyes.

"She's weeping from fright," Miri heard someone whisper. "Poor delicate creature."

As usual, Gunnar went into Jeffers's house to talk with him in private. A guard set Miri on the reed-strewn ground outside.

"Have there been more bandits on the road than usual lately?" Miri asked him.

"Rumors of them," said the guard.

"I'd like to return to Asland. If you'll escort me to the royal palace, you will be well compensated."

The guard shifted his feet. "I'm not going to Asland."

Not going to Asland? These traders always returned to Asland. Where would he be going?

Jeffers came out, and Miri examined him for any sign of disappointment. Had the girls succeeded? He *was* frowning, but then again he was often frowning.

The Lesser Alvans gathered with animal pelts, reed baskets and mats, dried fish, and other goods to trade and sell. Jeffers set the prices, negotiating between villagers and traders.

Miri stayed in the shade of the house, pretending to be recovering from her faint. Astrid approached and stealthily deposited coins in Miri's hand before leaving.

"Good work," Miri whispered.

"Shh," Astrid said, running off.

Miri counted the coins behind her back. Enough to purchase food for the next month and beyond. She leaned her head back and exhaled.

Miri had years of experience with traders, selling her family's cut linder stone and buying food to get them through the next season. Still, back home there was no robber village head, nor a scarred bandit lurking, possibly plotting to avenge the death of his chief. Miri began sweating as she strolled through the goods, selecting bags of grain, salt meats, cheeses, and other foods she could help prepare for the sisters, insisting on the same prices she'd heard Jeffers set. She carefully selected a fine pot of honey.

"Where'd you get that money?" Jeffers shouted from across the way.

The conversations quieted. Jeffers stalked straight to Miri.

"Are you addressing me, sir?" said Miri.

"Where'd you get that money? All of a sudden you have money on the very day that the mail—"

He stopped.

Miri stepped back, inching her way out of his shadow. "I brought money with me from Asland," she lied. "I've grown so tired of hunting that I choose to spend it on food for me and the stone house sisters. Is that all right? In Lesser Alva, can a person spend Danlandian coins to purchase food?"

"Of course you can," said a woman.

"I'll take your coin," said a trader, and others laughed.

Jeffers spit to the side. He leaned against a thick pillar of his house and watched her.

She glanced at Fat Hofer. His eyes were hidden in the shade of his hat, but he touched the brim, almost as if he were giving her an approving nod.

She quickly finished her purchases, and the girls arrived to help her carry them back to the house.

"I never see you speak to the other villagers," Miri said as they stepped off the reed island.

"We don't really belong to the village," said Felissa. "Our house sits on dry ground. And we have no boat."

"A Lesser Alvan without a boat is like a bird without wings," Sus said gravely.

"And we don't go to chapel," said Felissa. "We've never been invited."

"But Ma taught us the stories of the creator god, and we say our prayers," said Felissa.

They stacked the food in a corner of the linder room and stood back to survey the treasure. Even Sus smiled.

Miri asked, "Now may I teach you Poise?"

Felissa laughed. "Make me a honey cake and I'll sit through anything."

Miri laughed too, mostly because she felt uneasy in her belly and wanted to chase the fear away. She dismissed the feeling as surplus fear. They'd gotten away with their banditry. At least, Miri hoped so.

Chapter Ten

Night drops into the soul
Like a stone in water
And wind hides the ripple
Of the hole, of the hole
The heart bears the slaughter
The dry lungs tipple
The breath unrolls like a scroll

It was still bottomless night when Felissa's sharp inhale woke Miri.

Miri sat upright, rigid with sudden panic, and caught in the corner of her eye a shape in the doorway. Tall, perhaps a man. But when she looked, no one was there.

Felissa was sitting too.

"Do you feel that?" she whispered.

Miri shook her head no. She had not the talent for detecting emotions that the sisters had.

"Someone was really mad," Felissa said. "I felt so much anger, but you were all asleep."

"Maybe someone started to enter the house," said Miri.

"Or maybe I was dreaming," Felissa whispered.

Felissa yawned and lay back down. Miri stayed sitting on the reed mat, facing the door. If someone had been there and stepped onto the linder threshold feeling angry, Felissa might have felt it. Perhaps the intruder fled when Felissa awoke.

Miri's heart was fearfully pounding, easily keeping her eyes open. But an hour flowed by and the uneventful dark soothed her. As her heartbeat calmed, her eyes wanted to close. She pinched her leg to stay awake.

Sometime later she decided to lie down, just to get comfortable. She did not think she had fallen asleep until she woke again. The sky was barely lighter, the sun still a suggestion, an idea unspoken.

Miri rolled onto her back. With the coming of day the threat seemed to be gone, so when she heard a noise in the corner of the room, she suspected a rodent searching for food.

She turned to hiss at it, but it was not a rodent.

Jeffers had picked up her pack from the corner of the room and was headed toward the window. Miri nudged Felissa but did not take her eyes off Jeffers. Something glinted in his hand. A dagger?

He stopped, his gaze swinging to her.

"No one steals from me," he said.

The glint swung outward. Miri knew in that brief moment that seemed longer than an exhale that she should move. But she seemed tangled, trapped in a net of panic, her heart thudding away all reason.

He would have struck her, but a cord looped around his neck. Sus pulled.

"Support!" Astrid yelled, hooking him around the neck from the other side.

Jeffers raised his knife to cut the loop but Felissa struck him in the hand with a long stick, knocking the knife away and then thumped him in the belly to bring him to his knees.

"Here," said Astrid, handing Miri her pole.

Miri shook herself and scrambled to her feet. Even winded and kneeling, Jeffers thrashed like a caiman, and it took all of Miri's strength to hold her pole. Sus pulled on his other side. Felissa thumped his middle again.

Astrid climbed onto the roof. "Meat! We've got meat! Hurry! Live meat!"

Many villagers were up boating before dawn, hunting the night creatures, and it did not take long for someone to respond. Two men jumped out of their boat and approached the house with knives out, expecting to carve up a caiman.

Instead they saw Jeffers, thrashing on the floor of the linder house, hooked with two caiman poles.

"What are you about, girl?" asked a village man.

"He sneaked into our house, tried to rob us," Astrid said, hopping back through the window. "Four girls alone, and we caught him. I call for village punishment."

More had arrived now, looking through the windows and open door because they had not been invited in.

"It's Jeffers," some said, backing away.

"Doesn't matter who he is," said Astrid, loud and tall. "He's meat now!"

The villagers hesitated. This was not a stranger or even some known troublemaker. This was Jeffers tied up and doubled over. Whether it was sacred law or not, Miri could see they would never agree to execute Jeffers.

"Maybe we should just—" a man started to say.

"Astrid has the right to cut him up," Miri interrupted. She did not want to give the villagers a chance to excuse Jeffers or he'd keep harassing the girls. "But instead she'll show mercy. Banish him. Jeffers must leave on peril of his life. If he returns to Lesser Alva again, he's caiman meat."

"But . . . ," someone muttered. "But that's *Jeffers*."

Jeffers lurched to his feet, grabbing Miri's pole. He tore it from her hands and swung. She fell back, and the pole just missed her head. Sus pulled with all her might, Felissa struck him with her stick, but in his anger he seemed unaffected by pain. He snarled like a beast and swung the pole again. This one hit Miri, striking her on the side with a *whack* hot as a boiling kettle.

Astrid yelled, "Come in! Come in!"

The village poured into the house, laying hands on Jeffers, pulling him away. Still he thrashed, striking two villagers before enough men could hold him down. His violence seemed to make up their minds. Miri felt the moment when the hesitation streamed away.

"Banishment," Astrid said fiercely.

"Banishment," said a woman.

"Banishment," more voices echoed.

Miri heard pieces of conversations around the room.

"He crossed the threshold uninvited . . ."

". . . four girls at home alone . . ."

". . . swinging at that city girl . . ."

". . . banishment *is* just . . ."

The girls watched from the window as several men escorted Jeffers to the woods. He talked the whole way but did not fight back.

The villagers still in the house trickled out reluctantly, looking around as they went, as if they'd always longed for a chance to peek inside.

A young girl whispered to another, "Where do you think they keep their chest of gold?"

One woman paused by Miri. "Did he hurt any of you?"

"I'm all right," said Miri, rubbing her bruised side. "He was trying to steal my things."

"We caiman-looped him before he knew what we were about," Felissa said.

"Good girls," said the woman. She glanced around. "This room is emptier than I imagined."

"There's no chest of gold," Miri said. "There never was."

"I wasn't—" the woman started.

"Is that the rumor?" Miri said. "That the stone house sisters are wealthy? They fish and hunt like the rest of you. The only difference is that they live in this stone house alone, no neighbors to support them."

The woman nodded, her blush fading. "I didn't know your ma well. She kept to herself up here, didn't she? And you girls seemed to do fine after . . ." The woman sniffed. "Still, I should've come to say sorry, should've brought you food and checked to see if you were all right. We should've done something when she died."

The woman shook her head at herself and sniffed again before leaving.

Miri felt a strange tightness in her throat as if she would cry, though she was not sure why.

"I didn't know anyone in town even noticed when Ma died," said Felissa.

"They noticed," said Astrid. "They just didn't care."

"I'm sorry," Miri said. "I'm really, really sorry."

"Her name was Elin. And she had blue eyes and long, thin fingers and a habit of humming when she thought she was alone." Astrid spoke each word as though she could call up the memory into flesh.

"And she had a big laugh," said Felissa.

Sus's serious expression shifted to allow a smile. "I remember her laugh."

"Do you have a ma?" Felissa asked.

"I did once," said Miri. "I was born, and she was sick. She held me for a week and didn't put me down once."

Felissa lifted her arm. Miri shuffled closer and let Felissa hug her. It had been many weeks since anyone had held Miri, and the sudden touch made her feel even more the ache of absence. Sus and Astrid drew in, and the four of them stood together, arms around each other, hugging away the fear of Jeffers and the sadness of losing a ma that never completely goes away.

"Miri," Felissa whispered, "you don't have to ask permission."

"To enter our house," Astrid said.

"Not anymore," said Sus.

. . .

That night lying on her reed mat, Miri was as crowded with thoughts about Marda as the night was with sounds. Never before had she wondered, when their ma spent her last week holding newborn Miri, where was little Marda?

Miri had always considered that week with her mother the most precious thing she owned. She reached into her bag to retrieve her second most precious possession, the linder hawk Peder had carved for her. The head and beak were smooth, polished over time by the touch of her fingers.

I miss you, Peder, she quarry-spoke, her message riding the memory of their farewell in the palace courtyard. He was too far away to hear, but she kept quarry-speaking anyway.

I miss you, Marda . . .

Miri quarry-spoke the memory of the day she and her sister had explored the old princess academy building. A stolen afternoon, a giddy freedom, laughing voices echoing in the empty stone rooms.

Miri could not think of a memory she could quarry-speak that would communicate, *I'm sorry Ma died of having me and so abandoned you. I'm sorry I left you too.*

So she just kept quarry-speaking the happy memory, clinging to the linder hawk, in a swamp as far away as the moon.

Written Autumn Week Twelve
Never received

Dearest Miri,

This is silly, but I swear I heard you yesterday. I was pushing a cut stone up the quarry path when I suddenly remembered that day we walked all the way to the old stone minister's house, remember? The spring after the building was no longer the princess academy. We wandered through the empty rooms, and you acted out things your tutor would say. I do not remember ever laughing so hard.

Today that memory was as sharp as a stone wedge. But it had such a sense of you, as if I was not just remembering it myself but you were also quarry-speaking it to me.

I watched for you all day. I was so sure you were near. You did not come, of course. It was just my silly imagination.

Still, I went to sleep last night sure that you are well somewhere in the world and thinking of me.

Your sister,

Marda

Chapter Eleven

Katarina's scourge
Bloody, bloody war
Danland sings a dirge
Never, nevermore

As usual, Miri woke sweating. Winter was coming, but autumn still crackled hot, like embers spitting ashes, refusing to go out. They had a house full of food purchased with their bandit money, but none prepared, so Miri put some beans and water in a pot over the fire so it would be ready in time for lunch.

She trudged into the village and sat beside Fat Hofer. At first she thought he was asleep there in his same spot, leaning against the chapel, his eyes hidden by his hat, but when she placed a couple of coins beside him, he immediately snatched them up and tucked them under his blanket.

"Will Jeffers come back?"

"I doubt he's gone entirely," he said. "Late last night I saw a boat off toward the sea where no one hunts. But he would be foolish to attack you again."

"Sometimes men are foolish."

Fat Hofer grunted but offered no opinion.

"You'll keep an eye out for him?" Miri asked. "I'd feel safer knowing that you were watching our backs."

"If you pay me, then yes."

Miri smiled. "You'd do it anyway."

Fat Hofer lowered his cap farther over his eyes. He whispered, "Don't tell."

Miri patted his soft, warm hand and walked back, finding the girls in one of their usual fishing spots.

Knee-deep, watching for snakes and searching for fish, Miri took a calming breath. The breeze off the water smelled so normal Miri could not remember why she used to wrinkle her nose at it. The air was rich, thick, and full of life. Pleasant, even. How strange to feel as relaxed in this sticky, biting, crawling swamp as she might leaning back in a well-used chair.

"You like it here," Felissa said, moving in to swish a net beside her.

"Hm?" Miri said.

"I sensed it from you this morning in the house. Whenever you woke up, you used to feel disappointed, as if remembering again where you are and wishing you weren't. But today was different."

"I'm sorry, Felissa," said Miri. "I wish I didn't feel things so loudly."

Felissa laughed. "It's not your fault. Since you named it—linder-wisdom—I've become more aware of it. Or I listen more closely maybe. In that house, everyone's feelings are loud to me."

They sat on an only slightly damp patch of marsh grass. The sun rose over the swamp; the breeze was cool and briny. Dragonflies in shiny blue and green zipped, hovered, and dived.

"Ma used to call us the dragonfly sisters," said Felissa, her eyes following the dance of the insects. "She said we needed a second name, since we had no father name. She said we're like dragonflies—cunning and quick and sparkling like jewels in the swamp. She said it as though she was proud of us."

Felissa was still smiling when she started to cry.

Silent, she went back to the house. Astrid watched her go.

"When Ma died," said Astrid, "Felissa cried for days. She didn't eat, she barely drank. Felissa doesn't feel things halfway."

Sus was listening, head cocked to their conversation, and Miri suspected she'd been too young to remember those times well.

"In a way, it made Ma's death a little easier on me," said Astrid. "I was so busy trying to keep Felissa alive that I couldn't stop and feel—" Astrid took a breath. "I guess I still feel it, though."

"I'm sure you do," said Miri, "even if you don't show it like she does."

"Felissa feels something and it comes out of her," said Astrid. "At least she feels laughter more than sorrow."

"And more than gas," Miri said, hoping to make Astrid laugh. She was rewarded with a smile at least.

Astrid took up one end of her net, twisting new fibers into the holes. "In the village, families hunt together, eat together, on rainy nights sleep cozied up inside the same reed huts. What could Ma or our father or grandparents have done that was so shameful that the rest of our family wanted us far away where they never had to see us?"

"I don't know," Miri whispered.

Astrid shrugged and looked away, as if she had not really been interested in the answer.

The silence stretched, ticking with the buzz and click of insects, the swish of breeze and water, the loneliness of the sky. Miri filled it with a story.

She told of a bird born with its wings pinned to the ground. Each morning it struggled, trying to get free. By the afternoon, exhausted, it laid its head on the ground and watched the other birds soar.

One morning after a vivid dream, it felt more

certain than ever that it *should* fly. It struggled and struggled, and when noon came, the bird did not stop. The evening sun lowered, and still it grappled with the ground. When the first star pricked the night sky, a single pin loosened. With new hope, the bird pushed with more strength than it knew was possible, and at once the rest of the pins came out. The bird rose so quickly and so fiercely, it flew straight up into the black sky, where it became a star, never touching the ground again.

"Did you make up that story?" Astrid asked.

"No, but I can show you where it came from," said Miri.

Sus and Astrid followed Miri to the house, where Felissa had battled through her sadness to bring back her smile. Miri brought out her three books.

"This book of tales is like the one that taught me to read," she said.

"And the others?" asked Astrid.

"A history of Danland and a history of Stora, a kingdom to the northwest."

Miri fumbled with the books, feeling transparent, but no one asked why she'd made the effort to bring along a book about Stora.

Sus sat down and immediately started reading the book of tales, and for the next few days she was never without it. While they sat mending, fishing, or cooking, Sus would read to them, stopping often to ask Miri a question like, "What's a street?" or "What's a pigeon?" or "What's a mattress?" Miri would answer, and Sus would nod and keep reading.

"How did she learn to read so fast?" Astrid whispered.

"I think she might be really smart," Miri whispered back.

"You are noisy whisperers," said Sus. "It's just like, once you learn what call a wren makes, you can always pick it out of the swamp noises? Once you know what sounds letters make, you can tell the word, and once you know the word, there it is, making sense."

Astrid scowled. "I want to read too."

And so at last the princess academy began in earnest.

Miri devoted much of each morning to reading. Besides being a useful skill, reading tales introduced the sisters to hundreds of words unknown in a swamp but likely to come up in Aslandian conversation.

After lunch and a rest, they tackled subjects like History and Arithmetic while doing chores or fishing.

In the evening she worked on Poise and Etiquette.

"Can I please go read now?" Sus asked, walking back and forth while balancing Miri's boot on her head.

"Not yet," said Miri. "Watch your toes. In a long skirt

you'd trip stomping like that. Your body should make a straight line from your feet through your hips and up your neck."

"Who says that's the right way of being?" asked Astrid. She swatted her dark, matted hair over her shoulder. "What if I like how I am, what if I don't want to be Asland's idea of a lady?"

"The point of education is to learn other ways too. Don't just assume that all you know is right. Learn more and then choose."

Felissa seemed to float as she strolled around the room the way that Miri had taught. "I like how this feels."

Astrid blew air out of her lips.

"On my first day studying at the Queen's Castle, my tutor Master Filippus told us the story of Lord Aksel who listened," said Miri.

"Oh good, another story," Astrid muttered.

Miri pretended not to hear. "Lord Aksel's tutors and parents taught him Scholarship, Etiquette, and Lordship. But he also listened to the cook, weaver, farmer, carpenter, and all the workers around his estate. Other nobles mocked him as he sat knitting or planting seeds. But when he was called to lead his province to war, he didn't just know how to stab and shoot. He designed clever war machines for breaking down walls, knit traps, kept his army fed in a harsh winter. Lord Aksel became the greatest military leader in Danland's history because he studied much more than how to use weapons."

"You want us to believe that if you teach us this silly stuff, someday it may come in handy," said Astrid. "Mincing properly in slippers will help me sneak up on a duck, perhaps?"

"I'm saying you never know," said Miri. "Think of learning as storing up supplies you may need for a harsh winter."

"That's logical." Sus spoke the new word as if she loved its taste on her tongue.

Miri opened to the genealogy charts in *The History of Danland.*

"Those are your ancestors. Look, here's a Queen Astrid! And a Queen Felissa. Ooh, there's Queen Katarina."

Miri told them another story—though this time Astrid did not complain.

"Long ago a queen of Danland birthed twins. Prince Klas was the firstborn and so was heir to the throne. But before his coronation as king, his twin sister, Princess Katarina, forced the old palace physician to declare that she was actually born first. Half of Danland supported Katarina's claim to the crown, and a vicious civil war erupted. Neighbor butchered neighbor, brother fought brother, till Asland's streets ran with blood. Katarina was so enraged when her supporters lost that she tried to murder her brother on his throne. In sorrow, Klas's first act as king was to condemn his twin sister to death."

Miri abbreviated the story, because the account in the history book took its time, lingering over every detail, begging its readers to never forget the horrors of a civil war. One country fighting itself, like a man slashing at his own limbs. No borders to hide behind, no places to retreat. Just death and more death.

All due to one princess.

The girls were quiet, letting in the sounds of crickets and toads.

Then Felissa said, "Glad I wasn't named after her."

"They were right to cut off her head," said Astrid.

"I used to agree," said Miri. "Then at the Queen's Castle, Master Filippus taught us, 'History is written by the victors.'"

Sus brightened. "I see! We're learning the story from Klas's point of view, the way he and his supporters saw it happen."

"Imagine if Katarina had won the war and her children had inherited the throne," said Miri. "What might the history books say then?"

Astrid gestured dramatically. "After years of threatened silence, the brave physician came forward to reveal the truth—Katarina was the firstborn! But the evil Prince

Klas wouldn't have it and started a bloody war in an attempt to murder his sister."

Sus shook her head. "How can we ever know exactly what happened?"

"Historians read books, letters, and journals to try to unravel the mysteries of the past, but they can't be absolutely certain they've found the truth," said Miri. "For one thing, people change. What would you three have written about me the first day you met me?"

The sisters looked at one another and laughed.

"And now?" Miri asked hopefully.

Felissa put her arm around Miri's shoulder. "Now the story we told would be very different."

Something touched Miri's leg. A ladybug. She brushed it off as casual as anything, almost as if she had not been afraid for a moment that it was a snake. Almost as if she belonged in the swamp.

Written Winter Week Three
Never received

My dear sister Miri,

I have not written you for weeks because I had nothing to report. But today something amazing happened. A young man walked into the village. Yes, walked! He was alone and as dirty as a bandit. He is a large boy, broad with thick arms, but looked half-frozen and exhausted. When he spoke, all he said was "Frid?"

Doter went to the quarry and returned with Frid. When she saw the boy, her whole face kind of widened in shock that way it does. She called him Sweyn and asked what in all creation he was doing here. Sweyn just stared at her. Beside him, I thought our Frid looked almost average size.

Frid's brothers gathered, wanting to know what was happening. Frid told them that Sweyn had been one of her friends at the palace forge but she had no idea what brought him to Mount Eksel.

Sweyn walked over to Frid. He said her name again. And then he put his arms around her. Right there for the whole village to see! I would not tell anyone but you that I noticed how his hands splayed against her back, how he rested his face in her neck.

Of course her six brothers pounced on Sweyn like a pack of wolves on a hare and yanked him away. Sweyn started shouting, "I love you! I love you, Frid," over and over again. And Frid's brothers got madder and madder and started hauling him off. I nudged Frid and pointed out that that they were dragging Sweyn toward the Great Crevasse. That seemed to wake Frid out of her shock. She ran after and ordered them to let Sweyn go.

And then everybody just stood there, staring at one another.

Frid said she had to get back to the quarry. She started to walk away, and my heart seemed to stop beating. But then Frid looked over her shoulder and asked Sweyn if he was coming too. His smile nearly broke his face.

For the rest of the day, he worked beside her. They never spoke. But one time after she got a drink from the water bucket, she filled the ladle again and offered it to Sweyn. She held the ladle herself for him to drink, and you know what that means. You can bet Frid's brothers saw it too. They never took their eyes off Sweyn the rest of the day. I am sure Sweyn did not notice the brothers. He was too busy looking at Frid.

I am writing by moonlight as I do not dare use up our candles. But I am too amazed to sleep yet. A lowlander boy on Mount Eskel! And I think Frid means for him to stay. After all, she gave him drink from the ladle.

Your sister,

Marda

Written Winter Week Four
Never received

Dear Peder,

Letter writing is like quarry-shouting without linder. It leaves me but seems to go nowhere. I exhale wind, not words. I smile in pitch-dark.

I am failing. I would not dare confess that to Britta or Katar or Marda or anyone I write letters to, though they do not answer me either. I feel a tug from home, a hope that I might do some good and return to them their own mountain. And I feel a tug of expectation from Asland, that I can somehow turn these girls into princesses.

I am here, so I will keep trying to fulfill my duty.

I miss you. I miss being able to turn to you when I have a thought to share, and you laugh or smile or add a thought in return, and I know that someone in this great big world understands me.

Your Miri

The Forgotten Sisters

Written Winter Week Four
Never received

Dear Britta,

You may tell Katar and the chief delegate and whoever you please: at last I have a princess academy. It took a few months, a skinned swamp rat, three books, a great deal of cajoling and bartering, and one bandit attack—but do not worry about that part. I'll explain when I see you again.

I have sent letters to you with every trader group, but we were being robbed by an unscrupulous tavern owner and the traders in his pay. He is banished, so you should get this one at last. Please send supplies. We are quite poor. And perhaps a couple of trusted guards? The sisters were completely alone. There is no immediate threat, but with Stora across the border in Eris sharpening their swords, I cannot feel safe.

Even though much has changed here, I find I have very little faith in the mail. Maybe you won't get this letter any more than the others. So nothing I say matters, as I am probably just talking to myself. Ho hum, the moon is a plum.

Miri

Chapter Twelve

Ho hum, the moon is a plum
The sun is an iron kettle
The stars on their spits drip juicy bits
To sizzle on black sky metal

Felissa was leaning against the windowsill, and the breeze from outside rustled her honey-brown hair. Since beginning the lessons on Poise, Miri had noticed a change in Felissa's posture, a lengthening of her neck and a confident set of her shoulders. She did not seem to fit in the swamp anymore.

"'. . . and when he clambered over the first hill, he saw it,'" Sus said, reading from the book of tales. "'The house where no one wanted to live, bathed with silver moonlight. He ached with fear, yet—'"

"Traders," Felissa said, looking toward the village.

"Traders!" Miri leaped to her feet. "We'll have to finish that story later, Sus. Excellent reading."

Miri grabbed the letters she'd written and ran into the village. She kept slipping as she walked, eventually realizing it was from trying to skip. She traced her feet's inclination to skip back to a buoyancy in her belly, a raging hope in her chest, and up to the giddy idea in her brain that now that Jeffers was gone, she might get letters again!

The traders were laying out their goods in front of what had been Jeffers's house. Fat Hofer had informed Miri that Dogface ruled that roost now, but he tended to stay indoors during the heat of the day.

The trading party was a small one from Greater Alva, not Gunnar and his crew, who sailed in once a month from Asland. Even these traders had hired guards now. One kept whistling. Not a tune really, more as if he were practicing a bird call. The sound pricked goose bumps on Miri's arms.

No Jeffers, standing over the trading like the lord of the manor. Just Fat Hofer, sitting. Lesser Alvans asked him to barter on their behalf and then gave him a handful of this or that in exchange.

Fat Hofer was no longer slouching under his hat. Fat Hofer was smiling.

Miri gave her letters to the trader with the leather knapsack with promises again that if sent on a ship to Asland and delivered to the royal palace, they could be traded for coins.

"And here is a letter for you, Miri," said the trader.

Miri's feet bounced under her. She had not received a personal letter since her first trade day months ago! She gave him a small coin as payment for delivery. The folded paper envelope looked weathered. If there had been a seal, it was long gone.

Miri tucked the letter inside her shirt, keeping it silent against her beating heart.

She waited until she was alone—after supper was set to cook and the girls had left to go buy more peat for the fire. At last she tore open the letter and looked at the bottom, hungry for Peder's name, or Britta's, or Marda's.

But it was from the chief delegate. Any inclination to skip drained out of her. She scanned the letter.

". . . Delegate Katar reports she has received only two epistles from you, and Princess Britta, none. I hope the reason you have not reported back on your progress is that you are simply too busy schooling and polishing the royal cousins to perfection. When they meet King Fader, the princesses must shine . . ."

The princesses. Could he call them that when they were not?

The king and queen both had relations who lived in Asland and other provinces. Surely there were royal relatives of a suitable age who had already been educated. For the first time, Miri asked herself, why the Lesser Alvan cousins?

Perhaps because those other relatives would be known, their genealogy traceable. And royal cousins were not enticing enough to offer a king of Stora. Only a princess would do. So if there were no actual princesses, well, that conniving lot in the palace saw fit to dig up some obscure cousins and pretend they were princesses.

Miri sat on the stone floor, feeling too heavy to stand. If none of the sisters chose to marry a foreign king, Miri would fail Mount Eskel—and Danland too. But if Astrid, perhaps, agreed to leave home and marry Fader out of duty, then Miri would fail her and her sisters.

Miri missed home as if a rope strung from Mount Eskel were lashed to her heart, the distance pulling. She lifted her hand, pretending that Peder was there beside her, holding it. Her fingers closed over her empty palm, making a fist.

Miri crumpled the letter from the chief delegate and tossed it into the fire. She splayed her hand on a linder stone, aching to speak to someone who would understand. She quarry-spoke, praying her silent singing could find a chain of linder to carry it from Lesser Alva all the way up to Mount Eskel, to vibrate inside Peder and Marda and Pa.

She knew it was useless. Mount Eskel was farther away than even a hawk could see. And besides, the only stones in the swamp were in the house itself.

But she gripped the linder hawk in her pocket and kept quarry-speaking anyway, pouring memories out, trying to communicate her present with those who shared her past, who would understand, who loved her.

It was impossible. She gave up and lay her head on the stone.

The stone was cool and as smooth as water, as familiar as home. Instead of trying to speak, she listened. Not just with her ears. She listened inside, the way she quarry-spoke inside.

The idea of the redheaded twin girls playing with painted wood animals brightened in her thoughts. Miri startled. She was not asleep and so definitely not dreaming now. The image had seemed to come from the stone itself.

She pressed herself against the floor and listened harder, following the tail of that dream.

Thoughts zigged in her like a snake through the reeds. A first thought led to a second and a third. Quarry-speaking was never random. It had a purpose, something to say and in a hurry. So Miri thought, why not listen that way?

Quarry-listening, she thought.

Her head hurt as she concentrated. Not silently singing but creating a space inside herself for a song to fill. A new image burned in her mind: a younger Felissa and Astrid decorating their hair with purple swamp flowers.

She jolted upright. Where had that image come from? If someone had quarry-spoken a memory to Miri, it would nudge a similar memory in her own mind. Quarry-speaking never implanted someone else's memory. And this was certainly not her own.

Miri exhaled and closed her eyes, re-created that space of silence, and listened again for Felissa and Astrid with the purple flowers.

The image returned. She followed it to another, and saw Astrid and Felissa, perhaps having a race, leaping through the window, running across the floor, and climbing out the far window.

Another memory? But again, not her own.

The stone stored memories. When she reached out, trying to examine them as she might flip through a book, the images fled. She calmed herself again inside that listening space and followed the image.

A woman. Elin, perhaps, dark-haired with a round face and a very wide smile. She sits on the bare floor, playing a game of stones with a young Astrid and Felissa. Sus toddles over, knocking the stones with her bare feet.

Miri flailed for a moment, stranded between memories, but refocused, relaxed, and found another image.

The woman she supposed was Elin, standing, a tiny child asleep on her shoulder, a younger Astrid and Felissa clinging to her skirt. Jeffers in the threshold. He hands Elin a bag of something and then carries out one of her chairs.

Miri's mind swam forward and now witnessed baby Sus, face red from crying. Elin, her forehead wet with sweat. Astrid and Felissa standing outside, watching through the window.

Miri focused her listening to go earlier in time, deeper into the stone. Elin and one baby—Astrid perhaps—lying in a bed with a white mattress, attended by a serving woman, two armed guards at the door. Reed houses surround the linder house, perhaps the lodgings for the guards and servants. The room is full of furniture. A painting of a woman hangs on the wall. Miri almost recognizes the woman in the painting till something else distracts her—one of the guards is Jeffers.

Back. The house, empty but for a snake crawling leisurely across the stone, wasp nests in the high corners.

Back. The ground not so tilted, the linder stones tighter. Reed houses outside, an unfamiliar pale-haired girl inside, an older woman with a stern face.

Back and back. Glass in the windows, the wood door hanging straight in its frame. There again the redheaded twins, too big now to play with wood animals, sitting in chairs and cross-stitching like bored Aslandian ladies.

Back again. The stones being laid into the ground for the first time.

And then, Mount Eskel. The stones that will build the linder house cut from the mountain by people Miri did not recognize. Eskelites who lived long ago.

Miri clawed her way out of the memory and sat upright. She was wet with sweat.

She ran to the rain barrel and dipped in a cup, her hand shaking badly. She drank and breathed, concentrated on the feel of the ground beneath her feet, the sound of a bird shrieking across the water. The here and now.

Bricks of peat were stacked by the door. The girls must have come home and, thinking Miri was napping, left again. She felt more like she'd run up a mountain than taken a nap.

She found the girls out fishing and sat beside Astrid. A hummingbird buzzed from flower to flower, dipping its beak into the yellow, blue, and orange blooms. Suddenly one of the flowers seemed to reach out, grab the hummingbird, and pull it in.

"Whoa!" said Miri.

"Sly spiders," said Astrid. "They're big and the same color as the flowers they live in. The bird doesn't notice anything's wrong till it's dead."

Miri shuddered. She did not have a net or spear, so she picked some reeds and tried to weave them together. "Um, did any of the villagers help your mother when she gave birth?" Miri asked, thinking of Elin holding a newborn baby. In the linder memories, she had not seen a man who could have been their father—just Jeffers and another guard, always standing outside the house.

"I was young when Sus was born," said Felissa. "I don't remember."

Astrid did not answer.

After a few minutes Felissa went to see what Sus was grinning about in her book. Astrid kept looking determinedly down.

"Astrid, do you remember when Sus was born?" Miri asked.

"It happened in the night, I think," Astrid said quickly. "Felissa and I woke up in the morning and we had a baby sister."

Miri waited, offering silence.

Astrid sighed. "Ma went to bed one night with a flat tummy and the next morning she had a baby. I was not too young to realize that's not how things work."

Miri nodded. The linder house remembered. Sus was not Elin's daughter.

"And Felissa?"

Astrid shook her head, meaning she did not remember.

"You must be cousins at least," Miri said. "You're all cousins to the king even if you don't have the same mother."

"Maybe." Astrid bent lower over her net. "Or maybe we're castoffs. We're girls no one wanted."

"No," said Miri. She had seen the cast-off children in Asland—no parents, no home, begging on the streets. Orphan children were not sent to a linder house in a swamp. Only royalty could live inside linder.

And yet . . . the chief delegate called the king's cousins "princesses," but through the genealogy charts, Miri could not figure out how Elin was related to the king. He had no siblings, his only brother dying before he'd had children. Elin must have been a second or third cousin, but that still did not explain who the girls' father was. According to the stone's memory and Astrid's as well, Elin and the girls had lived alone in the linder house for the girls' whole lives.

A terrible possibility entered Miri. The chief delegate hiring Elin to be a mother, setting her up in the faraway house, giving her orphaned babies from Asland. In the absence of true princesses, perhaps he tried to create some, stolen from Aslandian streets and put away in the linder house of Lesser Alva like winter apples in a cellar, kept in storage in case they were wanted later. That keen-eyed, pointy-bearded chief delegate might do such a thing, but not King Bjorn—or at least not Queen Sabet. Surely the queen at least was innocent of the planned deception.

Would one of the stone house sisters be asked not only to marry an aged king but to lie about her birth as well? What if King Fader married a "princess" but discovered later that she was a fraud? Far away in Stora, what protection would she have from his wrath?

"Do you remember furniture in the house?" Miri asked. "Chairs, a table, a bed?"

Astrid looked up into the palatial clouds that had covered the sun. "I remember a bed, sharing it with my ma."

"Do you remember Jeffers being your guard?"

"No. There were others who lived in reed houses outside ours. But they left long ago. I don't know who they were."

"Servants. Guards. Perhaps they abandoned their duty and Lesser Alva. Jeffers stayed. He probably always collected your allowance from the traders and gave it over to Elin. Once the others deserted, there was no one to notice that he was stealing it instead. He joined the village, built his own house, and kept pocketing your allowance, a month here, a month there, eventually keeping all of it. Your mother didn't know what to do when the money and food ran out, so she agreed to trade Jeffers food for furniture."

"Until the furniture was gone," said Astrid.

"If she wrote to the king to ask about the missing allowances, Jeffers likely stole the letters. No one in Asland ever heard, and Elin must have believed that they'd just stopped sending it, that they no longer cared about her and her children."

No one from Asland ever came to check on them. The king's general disinterest in his cousins—or whoever they were—had made them vulnerable to a predator like Jeffers.

"Ma taught us how to hunt and trap," said Astrid.

"Perhaps she had to learn on her own first, since the villagers didn't seem eager to help. What a remarkable woman she must have been."

Astrid flashed a rare, sincere smile. Her chin lifted, her eyes brightened, even her freckles seemed to lighten.

Miri felt a surge of warmth in her gut, a surety for the first time since coming to Lesser Alva. Her mission became as clear as the swamp under a sunrise. She would not school and polish the girls into princesses for the likes of the chief delegate and King Fader. But she could offer them an education for their own sakes, knowledge that might give them armor against whatever would come.

Chapter Thirteen

⸙

Meat on the spit, and don't you know
Your lips are sweet, your voice is low
Meat on the spit, and don't you know
I'd swim a sea to be your beau
But meat's on the spit and don't I know
It's salted quick, cooked tender slow
Love in your eyes gives me a thirst
But the meat's ready so I'll eat first

Miri came in to find the three girls fighting. Not shouting or name-calling, but actually in a pile on the floor, throwing one another around, kicking and punching.

"Stop it! You'll hurt yourselves. What's the matter with you!"

From the pile of bodies, Felissa's face looked up. She was smiling. Of course that did not mean much.

Then Miri saw Astrid's face. She was also smiling.

"Get her!" said Sus.

The sisters launched themselves at Miri, throwing her to the ground. The hit knocked the breath from her lungs. Her arms and legs were pinned, and she stared up at them in hurt confusion.

"Come on, don't just lie there," said Sus. "Get free."

"I don't know how," Miri whispered.

Bored, Sus threw herself at Astrid, and the two began to wrestle, each trying to push the other's back to the floor.

"We've got to stay nimble," Felissa said, sitting up. "You never know when you'll run into a caiman . . . or a bandit!"

Miri tried to keep her expression still so as not to give Felissa warning before she sprang, but she quickly discovered that she was terrible at wrestling. Felissa pinned her over and over, and Miri could not stop laughing long enough to catch her breath. She crawled off to collapse in a heap of bruises, yet feeling good, bubbles of mirth and energy expanding inside her chest.

"I had something to show you," she said when she could breathe again. "Look! Your allowance! The traders gave the mail to Fat Hofer, he gave it to me, and I paid him for his service. No more Jeffers, no more banditry. We won!"

Along with the small leather sack of coins was a letter addressed to Miri Larendaughter.

"May I read it to you?" Astrid asked.

"Certainly!"

Miri had assumed it was the same bland note from a king's official that had accompanied their monthly allowances in the past. But as Astrid read, Miri felt her stomach shrink to a small, hard knot.

"'Miri, things are not good here.'" Astrid read slowly, her voice catching over some words. "'I cannot im . . . imagine you have had enough time yet, but it will have to be enough. There are—'"

"Wait," Miri said, standing.

"'. . . fur . . . fur . . . furious meetings and shouting and warnings,'" Astrid kept reading. "'I cannot go into details in a letter. But expect someone to come for you. Those girls better be ready, and just you pray to the creator god that the king likes one of them—'"

Miri snatched the letter from Astrid's hand and glanced at the signature: *Katar, Mount Eskel's delegate to the court in Asland.* Miri cursed herself. She should have checked first.

The three girls stared at her in surprise.

"Wasn't I reading it right?" Astrid asked.

"No, you were. Sorry," said Miri. "It's just . . . I . . ."

"You're feeling anxious," Felissa said. "You're sorry we heard that. You're very, very sorry, but—"

"Time enough for what?" Astrid asked softly. "What did you need time enough for?"

Miri exhaled slowly. When Astrid reached for the letter, Miri did not pull it away. Astrid finished reading.

"'. . . pray to the creator god that the king likes one of them enough to marry her, or all our work is undone. Be ready.'" Astrid scanned the letter as if reading it for a second time. "Ready for *what*?"

Sus frowned. "The 'king' refers to King Fader of Stora. Clearly we're being groomed as potential brides for him in order to secure an alliance and stop an invasion."

Miri gaped. "How did you—"

"I've read your books over and over," said Sus. "And I keep wondering, if you could bring only three books, why were two of them about history? *The History of Stora* and *The History of Danland*. Now it makes sense. You're arranging a marriage between Stora and Danland. Queen Sabet didn't have any daughters. We must be the next nearest unmarried female royalty, so we're being offered up to the king of Stora. If he likes one of us, then our countries are allies and maybe their huge army won't march in and grind us into the mud."

Sus spoke with no emotion, as if she were simply delivering an answer to one of Miri's teacherly questions. But Felissa and Astrid seemed too shocked to even speak. Miri took their hands.

"Sit with me? Please?" She led them out front, where they sat on weeds and leaned against the house, the breeze off the water smooth and cool. And Miri told them all she knew.

"What's the king of Stora like?" asked Felissa after a time.

"He's a widower, but that's all I know," said Miri. "This is why I shouldn't be the one to tell you all this! I'm sure the chief delegate could explain better—"

"You must know something," said Astrid.

"He's been married at least three times," said Sus. "The genealogical charts in *The History of Stora* show that. The first wife died a year after they were married. Childbirth, probably. The second died ten years into their marriage. The book was printed eight years ago, and at that time his third wife was still alive, and he had a total of sixteen children. Probably has even more now, if his third wife lasted long. And according to the year of his birth . . ." Sus looked up, calculating in her head. "He is seventy-two years old."

Felissa sucked in a breath.

Astrid stood. "We'll just say no. We'll refuse!"

Miri spoke quietly. "Yes, you could, I think. But the chief delegate has already written to King Fader and offered one of you to him. If you did refuse, he might be so insulted he wouldn't hesitate to invade and claim Danland."

"So what?" said Astrid. "Let them take over the cities, I don't care. We'll just stay here and keep hunting like always."

"Maybe," said Miri. A dragonfly had landed on a leaf right by her foot. Its purple body had an iridescent green sheen like a precious jewel.

"Miri," Felissa said. "All those delegates and royals and such in Asland who are in furious, shouty meetings, will they *let* us refuse and stay here?"

"I don't know," Miri whispered.

Sus began working it out, touching a finger as she made each point. "Danland offers us, Stora accepts, we refuse, King Fader gets angry, Stora invades Danland, we're *in* Danland . . . so, what does he do to us?"

For a while, no one spoke. Miri had not believed it possible for Felissa to look angry.

A call came from the village: "Meat! We've got meat!"

Felissa stood up, brushed off her clothes, and started walking toward the village.

"I could use some meat right about now," she said without looking back. "I could definitely use some meat."

Sus grabbed a couple of knives and a bag of turnips, and she and Miri hurried after Felissa.

"Astrid?" Sus asked.

"Go on," said Astrid, entering the house.

Miri hesitated.

"She likes to be alone sometimes," Sus said, following Felissa.

The village gathered around the house of a woman named Hanna, sawing off chunks of the white caiman flesh and sticking them on long green reeds. Several fire pits of large, flat stones lay on the reed island, the fire burning atop them, a barrier between the dry reeds and the flames. Children dumped buckets of water on the surrounding reeds to protect them from flying sparks, running to the island's edge to scoop up more.

The caiman was large, and the week's fishing had been good, providing enough food that Hanna turned no one away. Miri spotted Dogface and stopped by the farthest fire.

The mood was breezy and fair. Dogface passed around swill.

"Meat on the spit, and don't you know," Dogface sang out.

"Your lips are sweet, your voice is low," several sang back.

"Love in your eyes gives me a thirst," Dogface sang, sitting by a village woman, who laughed with her mouth wide.

"But the meat's ready so I'll eat first!" others sang back.

Miri had never heard this song, but apparently everyone in the village knew it—even Dogface.

Miri angled away from him, hurriedly roasting two pieces of meat before heading back to Astrid.

She stopped short at the door.

Astrid was wearing one of Britta's dresses. Peach-colored silk, it fitted at her chest, flowed out at her hips, and settled smooth as sand at her feet.

Miri took a step back, trying to slip away, but her bare foot made a soft sucking sound in the wet ground. Astrid spun around.

"Sorry," Miri said.

Astrid's cheeks turned red.

"It's a Storan design," said Miri. "That piece of white silk hanging from the front of the waist is supposed to look like an apron. The Storan noblewomen apparently like to resemble hardworking commoner women, except the fabric is silk, so they clearly aren't doing any work at all. It's pretty, though, and Danlandian noble ladies have started to adopt the style."

Miri pressed her lips together. She was in the habit of turning everything into a lesson, but right then Astrid did not need to know fashion history. Miri waited to see what words Astrid might offer the silence.

Finally Astrid asked, "It would be me, wouldn't it?"

"What would?"

"If Felissa married him, he'd tell her what to do and how to think and she'd just shrivel up. Sus wouldn't let anyone push her around, but she won't reach betrothal age for years. Anyway, I'm not going to let my little sisters marry some old man because I'm too much of a coward. But . . . I hate this, Miri. I hate it!"

"So do I," said Miri.

"There's a couple in the village, Ceki and Lans. When she was making baskets, he'd come up from behind to put his arm around her waist and kiss her cheek. When he went off in his boat, she'd watch him till he was out of sight as if she just liked the look of him. They had two little boys. When I was little, I used to play with some of the village children and wonder which would be my Lans. Then Ma got sick, I was taking care of my sisters, and I didn't have time to think about that. But even now I still catch myself thinking, someday I'll have a Lans. Someday I'll have a choice."

"You do have a choice," Miri said.

"Not really. Do I refuse King Fader and let him come for all of Danland and us too? Do I let one of my little sisters carry the burden and marry a stranger?"

"Maybe you'll like him."

"Maybe."

Miri had attended a princess academy. She might have married Steffan, who was a prince and a good person besides. But even so, she would have been miserable as his bride, giving up Peder, leaving Mount Eskel forever, becoming a lowlander queen. And what if King Fader was no Steffan? What if he was horrible?

"You don't have to decide anything right now," Miri said.

Astrid nodded. From nearby came the croaking of a frog, thin and raspy, like a sickly cough. The frog called and called and nothing answered.

Written Winter Week Ten
Never received

Dearest Miri,

The winter seems thicker than usual, cold and angry. Sorrow strikes Pa of a sudden, and he cannot hide tears fast enough before I see. I think your absence reminds him of Ma's. Peder's pa is still upset that he left. I worry that he will not approve your betrothal.

With no word these past months, I cannot help but worry that you are in trouble.

Sweyn is still here. His anvil will arrive with the traders in the spring, and he and Frid plan to start a forge. They go for walks in the snow. They hold hands.

Gerti plays her lute each rest day. The music is like sunshine. I have seen Doter fetch Gerti to go to someone's house if there's illness or sadness. I think about asking Gerti to play for Pa.

Esa is teaching the women what she learned of doctoring, besides running the village school. Something she said worried the village council. Since the king owns our land, he could take it back anytime he wants. The council talked of working harder in the quarry, trying to make enough money to buy our land from the king. But if he might sell to us, would he not rather sell to someone with more money than we could scrape together?

I do not understand kings and what they might do. But I do not feel safe.

Today I killed a rabbit for our stew. It was good to have meat. But. Well. You know.

Your sister,

Marda

Written Winter Week Ten
Never received

Dear Peder,

Lesser Alva does not understand winter. The swamp looks up at the clouds and laughs at the idea of snow. Nothing falls but rain, and thankfully we have a good roof and food stores. So in the rain, we study.

It is as if Sus was starving and just realized there was food in the world. She wants me to serve up everything I have ever learned. Astrid listens too but she still resists. I think she is afraid the prize for doing well might be marrying an old, thrice-wed king.

Felissa's mind works differently than her sisters'. She has not fully grasped reading, but the lessons on Poise and Etiquette come naturally. Despite a head full of snarls and muddy feet, I can easily imagine her holding her own alongside the noble ladies of the court.

Though you probably will not get this letter before spring, I imagine you reading it in your house by the window, snow to the sill. I am glad that you are home if I cannot be. Will you remember to slay the winter rabbits for Marda? I am afraid my pa will forget.

I am surprised by how much I miss a Mount Eskel winter. It is a relief not to be freezing day and night. But winter on Mount

Eskel is a deep breath, an extra hour, a pause, little work and a lot of stories and songs.

I miss you more than winter. You know that, but I want to say it again and again in case this is the time my words will actually reach you. I miss you, Peder. I miss you.

Miri

The Forgotten Sisters

Written Winter Week Twelve
Never received

Dear Marda,

My first day out here, a snake bit me. Every time I step into water since, I am flinching against snakebites. And caiman bites. I am exhausted trying to look for all the biting things.

All the same, I think my eyes have grown used to the normal movement of the swamp, as Felissa thought they would—ripples on water, flights of insects, breeze moving the reeds. It is easier now to detect the irregular movements that might be a snake or caiman.

I am so much less afraid than I was that I even learned to swim. The water is chilly—well, for Lesser Alva anyway. But my muscles warmed as I fought the water. Swimming is almost drowning but not, over and over again. I like not drowning very much.

I think of you every day.

Miri

Written Winter Week Thirteen
Never received

Dear Miri,

 If I do not hear from you soon, I will march to Lesser Alva myself. In all these months I have received only two letters from you and both were washed out with water, the ink running and mostly illegible. I know you were alive to write them but not much else. Surely if you were not well, the guards or servants of the king's cousins would travel to Asland to alert us. Still, I worry.

 Please write me a dozen times and promise the traders pure gold for delivery. I would gladly give them the rings from my fingers and the shoes from my feet, as they say.

 Though I do not know why they would want the shoes from my feet. They would most likely not fit. There, I have ruined a perfectly good idiom by being too practical. Clearly I am in need of my Miri.

Yours frantically,
Britta

Chapter Fourteen

A lost word of letters
Is no loss if not found
A lost letter of words
Is a loss most profound

Winter rains assaulted the swamp, wrinkling the mud, boiling the lake, thundering through the reeds. Entire days the girls barely left the little linder house. Whenever Miri ventured to the outhouse, she got well churned and poached. One slip in the thickening mud and she might have rolled into the turbulent and dangerous water. The rain, as Sus said, erased things. In years past, with no food stores, the girls had spent the stormiest days hungry, staring out the window. At least now they had food and books.

As spring broke, the lake rose up to meet them, lapping just a few feet from the linder house. The village islands drifted farther from shore. Snows and ice on Mount Eskel had begun to melt in the sunshine, dripping down, rolling through the hills and valleys, eventually finding Miri in Lesser Alva.

The longer the days, the more Miri's heart quickened. Surely time was running out. She did not know what information would help the girls the most when they left the swamp. After all, she'd had no idea that reading a little book called *Commerce* at the princess academy would change her entire village. So she just taught them everything she could think of.

"Master Filippus believes that three disciplines define us as humans," Miri said while they walked to the peat pits. "History, Philosophy, and Poetry. History is human memory, the examination of what came before us. Philosophy is human reason, or an attempt to make sense of what is. Poetry is human imagination, seeking to express what is, even while dreaming of what might be. History, Philosophy, and Poetry—that's what sets humans apart from animals."

"And animals don't wear clothes," said Felissa.

"Right, there's also the clothes thing," said Miri.

While cutting bricks of mud-like peat from the pits, the girls listed things people did that animals did not, including cooking their food, shaving mustaches, and refraining from sniffing one another's rear ends.

Dried peat looked and felt like dirt, yet it burned as

well as wood, emitting a scorched earthy smell. When she returned to the Queen's Castle library, Miri meant to research why peat burned. *If* she ever returned.

They lay their peat bricks on old reed mats and began to drag them back to the house.

"Miri?" A young girl with mud to her elbows ran after her. She pulled a crumpled, water-stained envelope from inside her shirt. "My pa found this letter in Jeffers's house. I think you can read, yes?"

Miri took the envelope. Her heart leaped when she recognized the handwriting.

"It's addressed to me. Thank you."

Miri gave the girl a small coin.

The girl glanced at where the girls were walking ahead. "Um, did the stone house sisters kill their mother?"

"What? No! Their mother had the swamp fever."

The little girl nodded. "That makes more sense." And she ran off.

In all her months in Lesser Alva, Miri had received only four letters: from the chief delegate, Katar, and on that first trade day long ago, from Peder and Marda. She'd begun to suspect that even with Jeffers gone, Gunnar the trader had continued to steal her letters. She could not fathom why, as she had coins now to pay for their delivery.

Miri tore open the letter. Reading Peder's words was like drinking cold well water on a scorching day.

Miri

I have been here for two months now and still no luck. I cannot get to Britta. But I am trying. I have to believe that you are fine, though I have had no word. I do not like that you are farther than a quarry-shout away. Please be careful.

Peder

Was Peder in Asland? And if so, why could he not get to Britta? What was happening?

Miri was so gripped by thoughts as she walked that she did not notice the newcomers in the village till she had nearly passed by the main island.

Among the reed roofs she spotted a glint of metal helmets. The shake of a bright red tassel. Three dozen tall men.

Soldiers. Katar had written that someone would come to fetch them to Asland. Miri surprised herself by feeling regret seep from her heart through her ribs like the mud between her toes.

But . . . Felissa could not read well, and Astrid refused to practice a curtsy, and none of them wanted to marry King Fader anyway, and if Miri failed, she would not win

Mount Eskel for her village, and the country would not be safe from Stora . . .

But . . . Peder was waiting for her. And Marda and Pa. It would be such a relief to turn her back on everything and run home after all . . .

But . . . the sisters. She would miss the sisters.

Miri dragged her load of peat back to the house, dropping it just outside. She brushed off her clothes and started toward the village. Why hadn't the royal guards come directly to the linder house? Most were talking to villagers on the main island, others punting in boats off the far shore. Suddenly one was chasing after a fleeing woman. He leaped and pulled her down.

The violence of the action shocked Miri. Then she registered the uniforms: close-fitting, hammered iron helmets with peaked tops; stuffed leather vests; round wooden shields crossed with strips of iron. Their beards were often black, but the hair on their heads was dyed yellowish-white, hanging long beneath their helmets. Those were not Danlandian soldiers.

Miri walked casually back to the house, forcing her trembling legs not to run and draw notice. The moment she stepped onto the linder threshold, the sisters hurried to her, perhaps sensing her confusion and concern.

"It's begun," Miri said. "The war. It's already here."

Chapter Fifteen

The dead cannot sleep long when the moon is round
The dead toss and turn deep in the muddy ground
The dead never rest well in the living house
The dead hear the secrets the owl tells the mouse

The four girls stood at the window, staring toward the village. The glint of sunlight on metal helmets was bright and strange among the reed roofs.

"We have to get out of here," said Miri. "Someone may have already told the soldiers you are the king's cousins. That's enough to get you noticed. And history shows that it's never a good thing when invading soldiers notice you."

She stuffed the flat bread they'd baked at the village's clay ovens into her bag, along with her three books and their remaining coins.

"We'll walk to the Greater Alva port. Hopefully I've saved enough to buy us passage to Asland. The king needs to know Storan soldiers are in Lesser Alva. And I need to keep you safe."

Astrid shook her head. "You used to say traveling to Asland was too dangerous, but now—"

"Now it's more dangerous to stay. Please."

Sus was wrapping her blanket around her shoulders like a cloak but Felissa just stood there, looking at Astrid.

"You don't want to go," Felissa said, her smile sympathetic. Her ability with linder-wisdom had increased more than her sisters', and she seemed able to detect even the subtlest emotions.

"This is our home," said Astrid. "Soldiers are just one more swamp danger."

"Soldiers are far more dangerous than caimans," said Miri.

"History is full of royals getting beheaded," said Sus. "And we're royal, whether we want to be or not."

"So we run off? Abandon our mother's house forever?" Astrid was speaking to Felissa alone. "No one in the village cared a handful of grain about us. Why should the soldiers be any different? We stay."

She turned up that last word till it was almost a question. Felissa's smile was nervous, her forehead creased.

"None of you are feeling very certain about anything," Felissa whispered. "Except Miri. She's afraid. She's seen, perhaps, what soldiers with muskets and swords can do."

Miri nodded.

"Felissa—" Astrid started.

"I think we should go," Felissa whispered.

Astrid blinked as if she'd been slapped. She wiped at her eyes with the back of her hand, grabbed the water-skin, and hurried to the rain barrel to fill it.

Felissa did not lose her small smile, but she took several deep breaths.

"We'll leave the letters and the painting and Ma's things in the attic," Felissa said. "Because we *will* come back."

Miri did not say how she too had left home determined to return.

They did not dare wait for full night. Surely the soldiers would come investigate the strange stone house. They shouldered their light bags and left the door, as always, dangling open on its warped hinges.

Trying to keep reed beds and tall brush between them and the village, they climbed the slope and entered the woods.

The sun was setting, and beneath the forest canopy night fell hard. In the absence of light, the noise in the swamp seemed deafening. Croaks and calls, rhythmic buzzing, high-pitched diving of flies and urgent, pitiable-sounding pleas from other insects. A nightbird singing, a screech, the crunch of something feasting. Miri startled at a squelch different from the rest. She looked back often.

She thought it safer to avoid the road, so they kept in

the trees, moving turtle-slow, scrambling beneath limbs only to trip over others. At that pace, they would run out of water long before getting out of the woods, and then there would still be another full day of walking to reach Greater Alva.

"Which way is the road?" Miri whispered. She was no longer certain if they were traveling in a straight line.

Astrid pointed. "Should we . . ."

"Not yet," Sus whispered.

"We're still too close to the village," Miri agreed.

They kept stumbling forward. Now that they'd left the swamp far behind, their passage was louder than the sounds of night.

"I think . . . ," Astrid whispered.

"Not yet," Sus said again.

But their slow speed was agonizing. Miri led them through the trees and to the narrow road. They'd only taken a few steps along the packed earth when a voice shouted, "Stop!"

Miri could feel Astrid tense to run, but she grabbed her arm.

"It's no use," she whispered.

The soldier reached them in moments, carrying a lantern in one hand, a buzz of light behind glass. In his other hand, a pistol.

"What are you doing out here?" he asked.

"Hunting," Astrid said. "Night is the best time for catching frogs. They shout out their location."

"Then what are you doing on the road to Greater Alva?" asked the soldier.

"Chasing a frog," said Sus. "Obviously."

The soldier glared, his frown lined with shadow from the bright light of the lantern. He looked over Miri's pack, the blankets they carried around their shoulders, and bags of food in their hands.

"Back to the village," he said, pointing with his pistol.

They followed him in silence. Miri was dismayed to see how little distance they'd managed to cover fighting their way through the woods. In minutes the path spilled back out onto the rise over the swamp. The soldier with the lantern whistled, a long series of notes without a tune.

Two more soldiers approached. The soldier with the lantern addressed one who wore a chain mail vest.

"Marshal, I found them on the road," said the soldier with the lantern.

"Runaways?" asked the marshal. Storan swords were as thick and as long as a man's arm, the hilts wrapped in leather, but the marshal's hilt was tipped with green tassels.

"They say they were frog hunting."

The marshal laughed. He had a wide mouth with lots of teeth. "Planning to walk to Greater Alva? We just saved your lives. You would have run out of water and been picked apart by coyotes."

How did he know so much about that small Danlandian path?

"You girls live in that stone house, don't you?" asked one of the soldiers as they walked that way.

He had a long, thin nose. Miri recognized him as one of the hired guards the day she and the girls had played bandits. When she'd asked for an escort to Asland, he'd said he was not going there. Of course, he'd probably paid the traders to accompany them. Disguised as trader guards, they could freely scout the area for Stora. Had any of her missing letters gone to Stora? What did the enemy know of the sisters?

"What is that stone house anyway?" asked the soldier.

"Rumor is it used to belong to the noble family of Lesser Alva," Miri said, thinking of the stone minister's house—the linder house that had once housed Mount Eskel's only nobility, long abandoned.

Miri could hear the soldiers slip and stumble, and the corners of her mouth twitched with a smile. Even in the dark, her feet knew how to avoid the deep parts, how much pressure to place on each step.

"I didn't think Lesser Alva was so rustic," he said. "I'd heard a branch of the royal family lived here."

"Does this *look* like the kind of place royalty would live?" Astrid said.

In Astrid's words, Miri heard the echo of her own tone that first day in Lesser Alva. *Why do you live here? You're royalty.* She blushed in the dark.

"Marshal, seems like a good shelter," another soldier said as the house neared, the white stones ghostly in the moonlight. "Those reed houses are built so low we can't stand up inside."

"It's far from the rest of the village," said the marshal, "but—"

"Yes, no one wants us too close," Miri interrupted, hanging her head sadly. "It's kind of you to walk us home, even though . . ."

"What? Who doesn't want you close?"

"The villagers," she said. "They're afraid."

"Of four little girls?" A soldier laughed.

"Well . . . you know about the linder house, right?" Miri said, thinking madly. "You have linder stone in Stora? You've heard the stories of a house built of linder where no one wants to go?"

"It's not so bad, sleeping in a house of ghosts," Sus whispered. "It's cold, but you get used to the whispering."

Miri bit her lip, unsure if Sus had gone too far. From the book of tales, Miri had read the girls a story about a house on a mountain where ghosts lived.

"Have you ever noticed how plugging your ears makes the whispers even louder?" Astrid asked Sus.

Sus nodded solemnly. "As if the ghosts were talking right inside my head."

Miri expected the soldiers to laugh, but under the moonlight their faces were stern. One gripped the lantern so tightly it shook.

"There used to be five of us, but our other sister never woke up," said Miri. "Though her eyes were wide open, she slept and slept until one day her heart stopped."

Two of the soldiers halted and just stood there in the mud, staring at the linder house.

"Looks fine to me," the marshal said.

The girls entered the house and turned to face the soldiers.

"You may come in," Astrid told the marshal.

Just a little closer, Miri silently pleaded. She glanced at the girls and knew they were also hoping he would enter the linder walls, where they could sense his emotions.

The marshal put his foot on the threshold.

"Afraid," Felissa said.

The marshal spooked. "What did you say?"

"You're afraid," Felissa whispered, so his soldiers would not hear. "That's what the ghosts are telling me. They say it's all right to be afraid. Fear is your heart telling you you're not safe, and a man should always listen to his heart."

That last bit was a line from the story. Miri pressed her lips together, fighting a smile.

"Afraid and thirsty," said Felissa, her eyes closed. "Your wet feet bother you, you have an itch between your shoulder blades that you fear is a spider beneath your jacket but you refuse to scratch it and show weakness."

The marshal backed out of the threshold, his hands in fists. "I'll knock this cursed place down!"

"And free the ghosts?" Miri said quickly. "The house holds them prisoner. We are the unwanted, motherless girls, condemned to sleep here and be their caretakers, and so keep them away from the village."

"Unless, sir, you are offering to free us from this burden and sleep here yourself?" Sus smiled hopefully.

The marshal kept backing up. "It's too far from the village. I have my responsibilities. Don't let me catch you near the road to Greater Alva again, or I'll dispatch my longbowman and ask questions later. You just . . . just stay here."

He cleared his throat and walked away, casting one

glance backward. The girls stood in the doorway, arms at their sides, faces void of expression, and watched him go as if they themselves were the ghosts. When he was almost out of sight, he reached his arm over his shoulder and scratched furiously at his back.

It was very hard to keep from laughing.

"That was risky," Miri whispered. "They might've killed us just for being creepy."

Sus shook her head. "They'll just think we're witches. Storans believe in witches and honor them—from a distance anyway. I read it in your book."

But that night Miri had barely fallen asleep when she woke up sweating after a dream. Again of the redheaded twins: one was crying, the other sullen in the corner. In the dark, her joke on the Storans seemed unnervingly real. The little linder house felt crowded with ghosts.

No singing came from the village that night. Only more tuneless whistling, like the call of some foreign bird.

Chapter Sixteen

In silence soul speaks to soul
As swans speak to the still lake
Merging swift and plunging past
No mark but the rippling wake

The next few days, Miri and the girls spent most of their time hunting for food while throwing glances toward the village. They stretched their stores of beans, peas, salt meat, and grain in case the traders did not return, but the thrown glances also took up a great deal of time. Miri could not help it. She felt as if there were a bear sleeping in the corner, and any moment it might wake up and notice them.

When Miri could stand it no longer, she put on her dirtiest and most inconspicuous silk clothes and walked into the village.

Soldiers were everywhere on the islands as well as one standing in the back of each reed boat, keeping an eye on the fishers as they cast nets and thrust spears.

But Fat Hofer was still positioned between Jeffers's house and the chapel, his hat low over his eyes. Inside Jeffers's house, Miri spotted a Storan soldier at the table looking over papers.

Miri sat beside Fat Hofer and set down a bundle of salt meat wrapped in leaves. He took it without looking and slipped it into the bag hanging around his neck.

"Has anyone told the soldiers who the stone house sisters are?" she asked softly.

Fat Hofer shook his head. "Few have ever known they are royal relatives. Jeffers made up stories to keep them isolated."

Miri met eyes with a curly-haired villager. He held her gaze a moment before squinting and looking back down at the reed roots he was peeling. All it would take was one person who did know the truth willing to exchange information for favors with the occupying soldiers.

"When the soldiers came, did anyone fight back?" Miri asked.

"Briefly," he said. "Their marshal held up his lantern and threatened to break it against the island."

Miri nodded. Loose fire would consume the dry reeds in moments.

"I heard them talk of Eris," he whispered. "My guess is Stora invaded Eris first and now Danland."

"You're not from Lesser Alva originally, are you?"

"Now that kind of information has a very high price, Lady Miri of Asland."

"I'll trade you my story for yours." Miri scooted closer so she could speak quietly. She told him about a mother who'd been fat with her and working in a quarry when she fell and birthed her baby early. She'd known she was dying, but her mother still refused to put her new baby down. The telling made the story almost tangible, a screen that enclosed them in a safe space away from pacing enemy soldiers. So she went on and described Mount Eskel, the princess academy, Britta and Steffan and bandits. She told him about Asland and the Queen's Castle and revolution. She explained how her whole self hungered to learn everything, but how all that knowledge stuffed itself between her and her home till she seemed so far away she was beginning to doubt she could ever return. And that thought nearly dissolved her bones into tears.

Miri finally stopped and waited. The story had no ending yet, and its loose threads shivered there, seeming to ask, what next?

Fat Hofer's jaw was stern, and Miri believed he would not make the trade. When he spoke, his words came quickly, his tone unusually clumsy.

"There was a girl from Eris who got with child when

she was young and unmarried. When her son was born without feet, her father tried to drown him, but the girl saved him and ran away. She raised her son on a boat made of reeds. Years later she drowned in a storm and the boat with her, but the son escaped a second drowning and crawled his way to the main village of Lesser Alva. He begged for scraps of food, waiting to die too. But he was good at listening and uncovered a hundred secrets that needed to be spoken." He cleared his throat and added, "The end."

Miri looked at the ragged cloth Fat Hofer always kept over his legs. She tilted her head, asking permission. Hofer nodded. She lifted the cloth. One foot was round and swollen; the other leg ended at the ankle. She lowered the cloth.

"My talent is hearing things," he said, "and I heard in your voice that your mountain is your feet. That's where you need to stand."

"Thank you, Hofer," she said. "That was a very good trade."

She leaned her head against his arm as she used to do with her father. After a moment, Fat Hofer rested his head on her own. Out on the water, a pair of geese escorted newly hatched goslings. They paddled about, disturbing thin lines in the water, and Miri marveled that they dared venture in the open at all for fear of caimans and snakes. She supposed there were always dangers, but the threat of death could never keep geese from the water.

A loud noise, some shouts from across the island. Miri stood, squinting against the glare of sunlight on water.

Two soldiers were dragging a Lesser Alvan man out of a boat. One struck him in the gut, and he doubled over. A third soldier turned to face the island and shouted.

"We warned you! All boats now belong to Stora. What did the marshal say would happen to anyone caught in a boat without permission?"

Another soldier answered, "Execution, sir."

"That's correct. So we'll waste no time about it."

Miri started forward.

"Miri, don't," said Fat Hofer.

"I have to—"

"Don't!" he said, reaching for her arm, but she ran.

They could not be allowed to just kill someone like that, and for taking a boat that was probably his anyway. Why wasn't anyone fighting back?

The soldier was removing a large flat stone from a fire circle. He placed it on the edge of the island. A woman began wailing.

"No," Miri said. The dried reeds underfoot felt as slippery as mud, and she seemed to move excruciatingly slowly, as if running through deep water.

Another soldier shoved the man down.

"No," she tried to shout. She could not make her voice any louder. "No. No."

The soldier pushed the man's back till his neck touched the stone.

"No!"

The soldier lifted his sword. Miri sprang.

She grabbed his arm. His other arm was already slicing the sword down. Something splashed into the water.

The soldier twisted and grabbed her, holding her tight, his sword beneath her neck. There was blood on the blade.

"What should I do with her? She's just a little girl."

"Wait till the marshal comes back from river patrol," said the other soldier. "See how he wants us to make an example of her."

From across the island she saw Fat Hofer watching. He would not shout no. He could not rush the soldiers. He knew, as Miri should have, that it would be useless anyway. The man was dead. And now Miri might be too.

The soldiers bound her wrists and ankles so tightly her fingers and toes tingled. She was so much smaller than the soldier that he simply threw her over his shoulder, carried her to an empty reed hut, and tossed her in. He stood outside, apparently keeping watch till the marshal arrived.

Miri leaned down, trying to reach the bonds on her ankles with her teeth, but she could not bite through. Her hands were bound against her back. She felt wave after wave of tightness in her chest, and she could not seem to breathe.

Behind her, a knife point thrust through the woven reed wall.

Miri scooted away as the long, jagged edge sawed through the reed mat. She was holding on to a frantic hope that she was being rescued when large hands pulled wide the opening and Dogface stepped through.

Miri bolted onto her bound feet and dived forward, trying to slam her head into his gut, a wrestling move Astrid had taught her. But Dogface simply grabbed her by her tied wrists and held her up.

"I know you," he whispered.

With all the fight in her, she could not even budge his hand. She kicked at his shins, but he did not so much as blink.

"I know you, girl," he whispered again. The skin around his long face scar was puckered, his left eye white. "I've known you all along. From the mountain. You killed Dan."

She shook her head, but there was no doubt in his expression. He was not waiting for her to confirm his suspicion. So what was he waiting for, an even more perfect moment to kill her quietly?

She stopped struggling and took deep breaths, looking out the door for someone to save her, knowing there would be no one. A scream would just bring the Storan guard.

Dogface had lifted her wrists so high, she was dangling. He set her down, bare feet to reed ground, and lifted his knife. She flinched as he leaned over and swiped. Her ankles were free.

Her heart was pounding louder than a swamp night.

"I like it here," he whispered. He was missing several teeth, and the tip of his beard was pale with dried mud.

"You like it here?" Miri whispered back, trying to understand his words. She'd been expecting something more like "I'm going to kill you now," or "Need me some stabbing practice."

"The widow Lussi likes me, I think," he whispered.

"The widow Lussi?" Miri repeated. Her head felt light as thistledown and nothing was making sense.

He nodded. "I want to stay here. Fat Hofer says you're a plotter. Always thinking. I want you to think of some way to fix this. Get rid of Stora, give us Lesser Alva back. Lussi loves the way it was, fishing all day, sitting with her feet in the water, singing as the sun goes down."

Miri nodded, her whole body shaking.

He cut through her wrist bonds. Then he took off his tunic and shoved it over her head. The mud brown cloth covered her dirty silk and hung like a dress.

Another tug and a swipe. Her braid lay in his fist. She looked at it and shuddered, thinking of a beheaded snake. Her now-shoulder-length hair fell loose, tickling her face.

"You're short, they probably thought you were a young child," he said. "And now you don't look like the same child who rushed the soldier. Don't run when you leave. And when you're safe—fix this."

He swiped some mud off the bottoms of his leggings, rubbed his hands together, and wiped them over her face. Without another word, he disappeared through the slit in the house.

Miri sputtered on mud. She stood there for a few breaths, feeling as beat-up and small as she ever had in her life.

You're a Mount Eskel girl, she told herself. *And down here, you're the Mount Eskel girl. So fix this.*

She slipped through the break in the wall and without looking around began to walk. She was tempted to scurry like a mouse, hang her head, dodge from shadow to shadow. But she kept her head straight and tried to walk with purpose—her stride long and confident, shoulders back, as in the lessons in Poise from the academy. A girl who walks like that has nothing to hide. A girl who walks like that is someone no one would dare harass.

Miri took the long route off the reed island, as if she were in no hurry whatsoever. Leaping off the island and into hip-deep water, she splashed through to drier ground. She did not head straight to the linder house but traveled through the tall reed beds to hide from village view. Caimans were rare around the busy reed islands, but the farther she walked, the more dangerous the turf. The sound of every slosh sent chills down her arms. Alone and knee-deep, she was easy prey for caiman or soldier.

She could no longer bear to walk casually. Tension was tight and singing inside her. She ran.

Felissa and Astrid were doing the washing outside the house when Miri stumbled past.

"What happened to your hair?" Felissa asked.

Miri threw herself inside, crouching low in the center of the house, out of view of the windows. The moment Felissa entered, her mouth opened, frightened by what she sensed from Miri.

"It's not safe here," said Miri. "And somehow I have to fix everything and I don't know what to—"

She started to cry, sitting there in Dogface's dirty

tunic and dripping mud onto the white floor. Felissa sat, put her arms around Miri, and cried with her, as if she could not help it.

Astrid brought Miri water to wash her face. Each time Miri pulled her hand through her hair, the abrupt end shocked her. Her first haircut, delivered by a bandit.

They stayed inside all day and ate cold bread. Sus asked Miri questions like "How far is it to Greater Alva by water?" and "Explain the tides to me." Miri could see no escape route. The road was watched, and the Storans had taken possession of every boat.

Miri did not think she could sleep, intending to stay up and keep watch. But the events of the day exhausted her and she fell unconscious moments after lying down.

She was in the middle of a feverish dream about running when a shout roused her. Miri stumbled to her feet, clutching the caiman pole she'd fallen asleep holding.

A figure was standing in the threshold, all shadow in the moonless night. Had Jeffers returned?

In a practiced maneuver, the sisters tossed pole loops over the person's head, binding his arms to his body. He struggled and called out, and Miri knew his voice.

"Wait!" said Miri.

It was Peder.

Chapter Seventeen

Take your time, sundown
Take your slow, sweet time
I'm not ready to say farewell
This day has been too fine
So wait around, sundown
And give me a bit more time

Miri tore the caiman loops off Peder and checked his face for lash marks and his shirt for rips. She wanted to just grab him and hold him and rest her head against his chest and smell his closeness. His warmness. His Peder-ness.

"You're safe," he said, gripping her arms as if he could not believe she was there unless he was touching her.

His pants were dripping muddy water, his shirt was stained, and his curly hair was stuck with bits of plants. She laughed and pressed his hand between her own and wished she had him alone where they could talk for hours and tell each other everything, everything.

But there was a panic pulsing around him. And soldiers on the islands. Dogface telling her to fix it, her braid in his hand. A sword stained with blood.

"How did you get here?" she asked.

"A ship," he said. "Stora seized almost all Danlandian boats. Some merchant ships that escaped have kept running trade."

"I imagine wartime trade pays well," Miri said.

"Exactly. The risk is high but so are the prices. So I found one of the black market merchant ships and persuaded it to bring me here."

Miri was about to ask how, but from his tone she suspected it was a long story.

"We had to travel from Asland close to shore," said Peder. "Nearly ran aground a couple of times, but we made it."

"I haven't heard from almost anyone since coming here," said Miri. "I tried to send letters."

"I didn't stay long on Mount Eskel. I was only home for a week before I went crazy with worry and told my parents I was going after you. I walked down the mountain."

"You did what?"

"Well, waiting for the traders would take too long. I was on my own for a few days before I found a cart man headed to Asland. You survived out here all right?"

Miri ignored the question. "You *walked* down the mountain. To find me."

"Well . . . yes," he said. "Wait—your hair! How did I not notice your hair?"

"Because there wasn't much left to notice," she said.

He fingered the shoulder-length ends. "When this is all over and you go back to Asland, those noble girls will see your hair, decide it's the new fashion, and cut theirs off too."

Miri laughed. "Ah yes, I've always been the height of fashion—and a fashionable height. The noble girls would cut off their tallness to match my shortness too if they could."

"They probably would."

Miri's eyes stung, and she realized she'd barely blinked, not wanting to miss his face for an instant. Peder was here.

"You two are sweet on each other," Felissa said. She was resting her chin on her hands, a smile on her face.

Miri blushed and took a step back.

"I can feel it, so strong," said Felissa. "Keep talking. Watching you two is like hearing those stories you make up—"

"Felissa," Miri said, warning in her voice.

"—about the boy who is sweet on the girl, only she doesn't know—"

"Felissa—"

"—because she's too busy learning at an academy, but he carves her a hawk out of linder. And they go walking together. And he holds her hand—oh! I love that story!"

Peder raised one eyebrow.

Miri's face felt so hot she was certain she was bright red. She gave Peder a stern look—a warning not to betray her.

Peder took her hand again. Then he put his arms around her. And then they were kissing. She felt her bare toes curl, her hand grip the back of his shirt. For a few moments, Miri conveniently forgot that they were not alone. When she peeked, all three girls were watching, mouths open.

"Are you two . . . betrothed?" Sus asked.

"Um . . . almost," said Miri. "As soon as we get home to our families."

"People fall in love in the tales," Sus said. "I didn't think it happened in real life."

Miri glanced at Astrid and caught the stricken expression on her face. Miri let go of Peder.

"Sorry . . . um, what happened when you got to Asland?"

"I went to the palace, but I made the mistake of meeting with the chief delegate before seeking out Britta and

Steffan. The chief delegate said your task was too important for distractions, forbade me from coming to you, and escorted me out of the palace. I tried to get a message to Britta and Steffan, hoping they would pay my passage, but I think the chief delegate ordered the royal guard to keep me out. So I stayed in Asland all winter working at Gus's shop, carving stone to earn my passage. I'd nearly enough saved when Stora came by ship."

"By ship?" Miri asked. Stora had invaded Eris by land, and the small country was brimming with Storan infantry just over Danland's west border. "I would have expected a land invasion."

"So was all of Danland. No one was looking for Stora to come by sea, and no one was expecting to lose Asland."

"But the cannons?" asked Miri. A fort at the mouth of Asland Harbor held many cannons, and in the past it had easily defended the harbor from sea attacks.

"Somehow Stora took the fort or else sabotaged the cannons before attacking," said Peder. "Asland depended too heavily on that protection. The Storan ships just floated into the harbor, unloaded an army on the docks, and marched into the city. The fighting was over in a few days. Storan soldiers have set up a camp in Commoner Park and a second camp on The Green."

"So they have the palace surrounded," said Miri. "The Danlandian army—"

"Is mostly in Hunter province," said Peder. "They were stationed on the border in case of a land invasion. The army's surely heard by now that Stora captured Asland, but it takes a long time for a large army to march. And in the meantime, Stora is laying siege to the palace. When I left, the king, queen, Steffan, and Britta were still trapped inside."

Miri pressed her hand to her heart.

"No," said Peder, guessing what she would say next. "I'm here to get you four to safety—*away* from Storan occupation. Leave Britta's rescue to the Danlandian army. Right now, your safety is my duty."

"So, we're leaving?" Astrid asked.

Silence answered. Miri looked at the little house, as empty as a seashell and white as the moon. About six months ago she'd barged her way inside only to faint on the floor. Now it felt like a tiny home, her own actions soaking into the stone, joining a hundred or more years of memories.

Felissa was gazing at Miri, and Miri wondered how much of her thoughts Felissa was able to untangle from her echoed emotions.

"I'm sorry," Miri said.

Felissa's smile was brave. She reached out to take Miri's hand. With her other she held Sus's hand, who in turn took Astrid's. They all squeezed hands at the same time, making them laugh.

Astrid looked up. "Creator god, keep Mama's bones, and the bones of our house. Keep our memories. Keep us together."

"Keep us," Felissa and Sus repeated.

For a moment, that little crooked stone house, its plain door open and warped on its hinges, seemed like the finest chapel. Miri's heart felt large and full.

"Keep us," Miri and Peder said.

He took her hand.

The girls gathered the few things they would take with them. Astrid set their extra traps and caiman poles outside the house so villagers would feel free to claim them.

"Oh," said Felissa when she saw them, and Miri guessed she only then realized they were leaving for good.

Astrid was the last to step out of the house. She laid her hand on the smooth white wall and whispered, "'Bye, Ma."

The moment Miri stepped out of the house, any illusion of safety crumpled. With no moon in the sky, the entire world was in shadow. Even swamp-born girls did not venture water-side at night. Things hunted at night, things with wide eyes that could strike true by starlight. Miri trudged through water sometimes rising as high as her chest. The brushing of water plants against her legs felt like the cold, smooth bodies of snakes.

In the direction of the sea, the tides were always changing the land. There was no path to memorize, no sure way. But that was where Peder had hidden the small boat he had rowed from the merchant ship.

On the village islands, fires glowed from lanterns. Voices murmured, buzzing low over the water like dragonflies. Since the Storan soldiers had come, playful night music no longer called out from the village.

But tonight someone sang—deep and sad, a ballad of endings. *"I'm not ready to say farewell, this day has been too fine. So wait around, sundown, and give me a bit more time."*

"That's the truth," Astrid whispered.

Fat Hofer was likely still sitting with his back to the chapel, looking dull and uninterested so that the Storans would not bother about him, and yet always paying attention. Maybe he noticed the hearth fire extinguished in the linder house and guessed what they were doing. Maybe he was, in his way, saying good-bye.

"Good-bye, Hofer," Miri whispered.

She felt a sting of guilt, but she was no help to him

trapped in Lesser Alva. *Fix this*, Dogface had said. She had to leave to try. Last in line, she dragged herself a little faster through the thick water, trying to catch up with the others.

Something sploshed behind her. Miri's heart startled like a frog. Her feet, already cold from the water, felt hard as ice.

"Are we near your boat?" she whispered to Peder.

"I think so," he whispered back. "I wasn't sure if the Storans had set guards by your house, so I didn't dare drag the boat too close. I tied it to some reeds. I can't see it . . ."

He poked one of the sharpened sticks they had brought from the house into the reed beds, hoping to hit the hardness of the hidden boat. Sus, Felissa, and Astrid had sticks as well. They fanned out from Peder, sweeping the surface of the black water.

Miri stayed put. Till they found the boat, there was no use moving more than needed and risking falling into a pit. Or rustling in the water and attracting predators. Everywhere she looked, the glimmer of starlight on water resembled eyes. After a few moments she could hear Peder sweeping for the boat but no longer see his shape.

Again the sploshing. It sounded more definite, rhythmic. Had someone followed them out? A troop of soldiers would make more noise.

Another definite splash.

"Did you hear that?" Miri whispered.

But the girls were no longer near enough to hear her.

Miri stared into the dark, willing the vague shapes into forms that would make sense. A shadow sliding toward her. A boat, someone punting. Starlight touched his eyes. Jeffers.

Their noise had attracted a predator indeed.

Miri's scream caught in her throat, afraid of Jeffers, afraid of alerting the soldiers, too afraid to move.

"My town," Jeffers snarled. "My territory! You're the thief. I've got meat here!"

He lifted his pole and the barbed, forked end glinted. A fishing spear. The water felt like stone around her legs, the mud beneath sucking at her feet. She held no stick. She could not run.

There was nothing between her and his spear except a sharp, crackling sound and a brief burn of light.

Jeffers hunched over, a gurgle crawling out of his throat. He dropped the spear. His eyes looked beyond Miri, and then he fell facedown in the water.

Miri shoved both hands against her mouth to stifle the scream finally rising. She backed away and into Peder. He was holding a pistol.

"It worked it worked it worked," Peder was mumbling.

"It's so wet out here I didn't know if the gunpowder was ruined I didn't know I'm sorry I'm sorry."

Peder dropped the pistol into the water. He did not take his eyes away from Jeffers. Miri hugged him tight, wanting him to feel her warmth. She put her hands on his face and looked at him till he pulled his gaze from Jeffers.

"He would have killed me," she said.

Peder exhaled very slowly. "I'd do it again, Miri. Of course I would. And it was the right thing to do. I know."

"But . . . ," she said.

"But I don't want to. You . . . you're a warrior, I think. In a way, you are. But I'm not. I don't want to be that kind of a person."

She nodded.

Astrid moved toward them, pulling the low, flat boat. It was painted black and made of wooden planks, not reeds—clearly not of Lesser Alva.

"We should go," she said, her voice tight. Surely the noise from the pistol would attract the soldiers.

Miri climbed into the boat after Sus, her muscles trembling with the slight effort, already spent with fear. There had been warning in Astrid's tone, and Miri realized she was worried about more than soldiers. Jeffers's blood would attract caimans.

They used their sticks to push against the ground through the waters. It was unbearably slow. The clawing tips of plants tugged at them, and unexpected rises in land would make the boat come to a stop, and they would all have to get out and drag it back into water.

Boats with lanterns were already sliding around the area where Peder had shot Jeffers.

As soon as they entered water deeper than the sticks, Peder took the one oar and rowed them out to open water. He sat at the bow, his arms and shoulders working stroke after powerful stroke.

"I can take a turn," Miri whispered.

Peder shook his head and kept rowing. Miri thought he needed something to do with his arms just then, some way to use his strength that was not destructive.

He moved them around the last of the fingers of marshland and toward the open channel of the sea. The water finally became smooth under the starlight—no more reeds or water plants. The smell of it changed too— briny, sharp, cold, less alive. Miri faced backward, keeping an eye on the pricks of light that might be soldier-held lanterns. Then the night swallowed those too, and Miri could see nothing of Lesser Alva. All she could hear was the splash of the oars and Peder's breathing, hard and dry.

After a time, Miri turned around and spotted a new

point of light directly ahead. Her heart rattled in her ribs. Had the Storans chased them from the other side? But Peder pulled in the oar, letting the boat drift, and made three soft, throaty calls.

Over the water rode the answer, as exact as an echo.

Peder rowed on. When they reached the single light, Miri saw it belonged to a lantern dangling over the side of a ship. A crew of faces stood at the railing.

Someone extinguished the lantern, and hooked ropes tumbled down. Peder attached them to the rowboat, and the ship's crew pulled the girls up. Hands took Miri's arms and waist and helped her out of the rowboat and onto the deck.

A ship full of men, none in uniform, most with pistols, all with sabers. No country flag flying. Miri choked on an inhale. Peder had brought her aboard a pirate ship.

Chapter Eighteen

Have you ever seen a girl in red?

Yes, I've seen a girl in red

With long black curls upon her head?

High lo, there she goes now

Have you ever seen so swift a sail?

Yes, I've seen so swift a sail

With a mermaid carved upon her bow?

High lo, there she goes now

Miri gasped too loudly and several voices hushed her. They'd left the reed islands far behind but were nowhere near safety. Not with Storan ships patrolling the coast. Not with war churning.

A man Miri assumed was the captain made some signal with his hand, and his crew secured the rowboat and pulled up the anchor. The sails opened, the ship lurched forward, and the sisters grabbed for the railing to keep from falling.

A ship operating under no country's flag. Against the rule of law. In wartime. For gain.

"Peder," Miri said softly. "These are . . ." She did not say *pirates*, but Peder nodded, hearing the word anyway. His smile was extremely pleased.

The captain approached them, adjusting his three-cornered hat. His beard was black and ragged, and his clothes cut from some light fabric as if he did not feel the chill ocean breeze that burrowed right through Miri's still-damp dress. Peder introduced him as Captain Bodel.

"So this is the treasure," he said, looking Miri over with narrowed eyes. "Are you worth all this trouble?"

Miri shook her head.

Felissa and Sus both yawned at the same time.

"We'd better get the *ladies* settled," said the captain, as if the word was a joke. "They will take my cabin."

"That's very kind," said Miri.

"I suppose it's very kind of my employer, as it was his order," said Captain Bodel.

The girls followed Peder down the ladder into the hold. The captain's cabin was almost as short as it was narrow. His small bed was secured to the floor. Two hammocks hanging from hooks on the ceiling took up the rest of the space. Felissa climbed into a swinging hammock, Sus curled up in the bed, and both fell asleep. Miri put down her pack but was too anxious to rest. Peder could never afford to hire a boat and crew to rescue her.

Surely the king could, but the captain had assumed that Miri herself was the "treasure," not the royal cousins.

When she left the cabin, Astrid was washing her face using water from a barrel.

Miri climbed back up the ladder. The ship was a small cargo vessel, a merchant's ship used for ferrying goods up and down the coast. But the sails were large, the ship moving at a speed that took her breath away. She joined Peder at the bow.

"Who is the captain's employer?" she whispered.

"Um," said Peder.

"Who," said Miri.

"I, uh . . ."

"You're clearly trying to think of a way to distract me from the question, but you're a terrible liar, so just give up."

Peder frowned. "Timon."

Miri gasped again. Timon had been a friend to her once—or she'd thought so at the time. But he'd lied and manipulated her for his own purposes. She may have forgiven him, but she certainly did not trust him.

"I didn't want to go to him either," said Peder, "but I'd run out of options. He's wealthy, he had access to his father's ships, and he was willing."

A tightness around Peder's mouth indicated there was something he was holding back.

"What?" Miri asked. "What else?"

"Timon said his father and other merchants had been in talks with the chief delegate about buying Mount Eskel and taking over the quarry."

The ship hit a large wave, and the bow thrust into the air, falling till it slammed onto water. Salty spray shot across Miri's face. Her breath seemed to have fallen out again, left tumbling into the ocean.

"Already?" she squeaked.

"Timon's condition for lending me this boat was that, when the war is over, he gets to meet and negotiate with you himself for Mount Eskel's quarry."

Miri blotted the water from her face. When she spoke, she was amazed that she did not scream. "I can't . . . I can't think about Timon and the quarry right now. I can't think about another thing."

Peder nodded and was silent for a time.

"This ship was docked in Fuska when Stora took Asland. Timon thought it our best bet to avoid capture because it was built from a Storan design. I traveled by land from Asland to Fuska's harbor, and we sailed at night. By luck, no patrol ships have seen us."

"Well, as soon as we get back to Asland—"

"No," Peder said. "We're taking you away. Timon has friends across the channel. He said we can stay there till after the war."

"My family is in Danland. And Britta! Britta and

Katar and Steffan are trapped in that palace. I can't leave them."

"If you won't worry about your own safety," said Peder, "think about these girls, who—"

"Who just might be the answer. That's why we need to get them to Asland before the Danlandian army returns to fight. We need to negotiate with Stora and give the plan a chance."

Peder turned to look at her fully. "You would turn them over to Stora so their king could have his pick of brides?"

"I know," Miri whispered. "Sometimes I wonder what's the matter with me. But . . . but they know about it now. Astrid agreed to just *meet* King Fader, and if he's not too horrible, for the sake of Lesser Alva and Danland and her own sisters' safety, she might be willing . . ."

"What if it was *you* King Fader wanted to marry?" Peder said. His blue eyes looked purple in the starlight.

"But it's war, Peder." She rubbed her eyes, a dozen memories colliding behind her lids—musket shots, bodies crumpling, Peder struck by a pistol bullet, the Storan soldier's sword falling onto the boatman's neck. "Shouldn't we do anything we can to stop a war?"

"Sometimes I think we should do anything we can just to get back home."

Captain Bodel strolled over, his thumbs in his sword belt. Miri startled upright, suddenly aware she and Peder had been speaking so close that their foreheads had nearly touched.

"Not sleepy, my lady?" Captain Bodel said, raising an eyebrow, his eyes taking in her whole self.

This ship felt as safe as a nest of snakes.

"Thank you for coming for us, Captain," she said.

"My employer was *eager* to save you. I'd love to know why." The captain scratched his bearded chin, his dark eyes never leaving Miri.

She glanced at Peder, who was frowning.

"Captain," a breathless sailor called. "Captain, I see something off the port bow."

"A ship?" he asked.

"If it is, it's running dark," said the sailor.

Captain Bodel, Miri, and Peder followed the sailor to the port railing. The sky was cloudy above the horizon, and Miri could not tell where the sea ended and the sky began. But she noticed one space in the darkness that shifted. Moved toward them. Moved fast.

The captain was peering through a spyglass.

"It's probably a first-rank ship," he said. "Three gun decks, at least eighty cannons. We can't outrun her and certainly can't outgun her."

"How many cannons do you have?" Miri asked.

The captain closed his eyes and touched his fingertips as if counting a high number. "Uh . . . two."

"A Storan or Danlandian ship?" Miri asked, though the coldness in her belly told her she already knew.

"The only ships running in this part of the channel are Storan or pirate," said a sailor.

At the captain's command, another sailor climbed the mast and clipped something to its top. The wind snapped at it, and Miri recognized the green field and crossed daggers of the Storan flag.

"One flag won't fool them," Miri said.

"Well, one's all we have," said the captain. "Peder, be ready to fetch that fancy paper my employer drew up for you and pray to the creator god that it works."

"Why don't we at least try to run?" Miri asked.

No one answered, as all attention was on the looming black shape. The silence seemed to contain the answer. If they ran, the ship would follow. And fire. And send them all down into the blackness.

The captain called out orders, and sailors lowered the sails. The ship drifted, slowing against the waves. The loss of speed panicked Miri's blood. How could they bear to just sit here and wait?

The great ship came up beside them, its broadside

facing theirs. A voice from the darkness called out a warning Miri did not understand, but the sailors on the pirate boat did. They backed away to the starboard side, so Miri and Peder followed.

Hooks came flying out of the dark, grabbing the port railing. Unseen sailors pulled the hooked ropes, and the small ship moved till both ships were nearly touching. The pirate ship looked like a puppy beside a horse. Miri leaned her head back, failing to glimpse even the Storan ship's upper deck.

Sailors descended the ropes, with swords in scabbards and pistols in their belts.

Lastly, a man in a fine uniform climbed down. He wore a close-fitting iron helmet like the Storan soldiers, though his peaked higher, and red fringe topped the hilt of his sword. His beard was black streaked with gray, his hair bleached pale blond.

"Name yourself," he said in a loud, precise voice.

"I am Captain Bodel," their captain said with a short bow. "We're a cargo vessel, sir, as you can see, but we received orders from General Jons to run this route. He said extra eyes for Stora are always needed."

"And why are you running dark and so close to the shore?" the Storan captain asked.

"Running dark was a precaution, sir," said Captain

Bodel. "I didn't want to be spotted by rebel Danlandian ships. We're small, as you see, and with few defenses."

The Storan captain nodded. These were the responses he was expecting. But then he held out his hand and said, "Papers."

There was the slightest hesitation, but Captain Bodel said, "Of course," and nodded at Peder, who descended to the cabin.

Papers. Those would be official, signed and stamped documents from the Storan naval commander commissioning Captain Bodel's ship into the Storan wartime navy—proof that this boat was what it claimed to be.

But it was not. So whatever papers Peder had gone to fetch would be fakes.

Miri stared at the great wall of ship beside them, the black eyes of cannons staring back, and tried not to imagine what would happen when this commander discovered Captain Bodel's story was a lie.

There was motion at the ladder, but it was not Peder who emerged through the hole.

"What is all the bother?" Astrid asked, her voice flutey.

Astrid was wearing one of Britta's dresses—the fine peach silk with a white silk apron in the Storan style. It was wrinkled from being stuffed in a bag, but the wrinkles were hard to spot in the starlight. She'd pinned up her hair to hide the snarls, and her face and hands were well washed. But most striking was her posture—shoulders back and down, spine straight, hands held modestly before her middle. Her chin was raised and she looked around as if at inferiors.

Miri blinked. And then she curtsied. "Um, my lady, you shouldn't trouble yourself."

"Who are you?" the Storan captain asked Astrid.

Miri took a long breath while trying to think. "It is vulgar to ask a lady to identify herself." She curtsied to Astrid, backed away, and then spoke in a low polite tone, as if for the captain's ears alone. "Her Grace, Princess Helka Appaluna of House Stora. She has been summoned to Asland."

There was, in fact, a Princess Helka Appaluna, one of King Fader's many daughters. Miri had read her name on the Storan genealogical charts. If the Storan captain had ever met the princess, the farce would fail. As it would if he had any opinions about how a proper lady's maid should dress. With great effort, Miri resisted smoothing her wind-tangled hair or adjusting her skirt, dried stiff from seawater.

The Storan captain narrowed his eyes at Captain Bodel, waiting for him to speak. Miri held her breath.

"Apologies, sir," said Captain Bodel. "I would have mentioned the princess at once, only her presence here is secret, as you can understand. But now that you've met her, you understand our stealth and need to get quickly to Asland."

Astrid held her chin up as she spoke. "Gentlemen, you do realize it is *night*? I was attempting to relax in my quarters. Perhaps you could trouble yourself with a few manners and keep the ruckus down."

She turned and started back down. Miri followed like a helpful maid, taking her hand as she descended the ladder.

Once they were in the dark of the hold, Miri could hear Astrid let out a shaky breath.

"How—" Miri whispered.

"I paid attention during Poise lessons," Astrid whispered.

"You could have fooled me."

Peder came from deeper within the hold, a box in his hand. "What—"

Miri held up a hand to stop him and pressed a finger to her lips.

They looked up, listening through the boards. There were footsteps, some murmurs, and then the Storan captain's clear voice. "My ship is better equipped to house royalty than this little sloop."

"I wish she would go with you," said Captain Bodel. "To be frank, Her Grace is the most difficult cargo I've ever carried."

The Storan captain laughed. "That I can believe."

"But the general reminded me of that wise adage: A woman on a warship is like a crack in its keel."

The Storan captain laughed again.

"I gathered the general would rather transport her in a cramped cargo vessel than bring bad luck to a vital ship such as yours."

"And I thank him for it," said the Storan captain. "But such a treasure should be well guarded. Sail in our wake. We will see you to Asland."

The Storan captain barked some orders. Miri heard boots cross the deck and then a scrambling sound as if men were climbing back onto the warship. After a few minutes, their ship lurched forward, the sails full of wind again.

"You'd better stay in your quarters, Princess Helka Appaluna," Miri said to Astrid.

Miri and Peder climbed back up to the deck. She'd been about to ask a question, but a look from Captain Bodel silenced her. A dozen soldiers from the Storan ship had remained on their deck.

Miri slowed, smiling as if nothing was wrong in the world. She ambled to the bow, Peder beside her.

"There's no escaping across the channel now," Miri said quietly.

Peder shook his head.

From behind a cloud, a thin moon uncurled, barely brighter than the stars.

The water was sky-black, each lift and bend reflecting a fragment of the moon, as if the sea too were full of stars. The ship slowed, following the Storan vessel toward the open sea, caught the wind again, and pushed forward with a jolting speed. Looking back, she could no longer spy any land. She'd never felt so far away from home. Her legs trembled, missing again the stone mountain underfoot. It seemed for a moment that there was nothing but dark and stars and wind.

Peder took her hand.

Chapter Nineteen

Some shade from the sun would be glad
A plate of hot roast would be glad
A kiss from a girl would be glad
Out here on the surging sea
If I kissed you would you be mad?
Out here on the surging sea

For the rest of the voyage, Astrid remained Princess Helka Appaluna. At first she hid in the captain's cabin. But the motion of the ship rocked her stomach, and she became so ill she could not keep down even water. So Miri prepared them all to be seen by daylight. They washed their hair with a block of the rough kitchen soap, rubbed it with cooking oil, and painstakingly combed out the snarls. Felissa trimmed and cleaned Astrid's fingernails, Sus worked the wrinkles out of the silk dress, and all reviewed Miri's lessons on Poise and Etiquette.

"I thought learning to curtsy properly was a kind of

game," Felissa said. "Who knew our lives might depend on it?"

Felissa smiled. Astrid did not.

At last Astrid emerged on the deck. Miri brought her a stool so she could sit by the railing, and her sisters acted as her maids, standing nearby. Astrid stared at the swelling water and seemed to concentrate on not revisiting her breakfast.

Miri was now a maid to Princess Helka. Peder was a sailor to Captain Bodel. They had only stolen moments together.

"Stora always paid rent to Eris to use their harbor," Miri whispered as they sat in the galley chopping potatoes. "Why did they invade now?"

"Maybe they grew sick of paying rent," said Peder.

"Maybe," she said. "And once Eris fell so easily, they had this whole big army armed and ready and thought, 'Well, Danland is nearby' . . ."

"I don't like this," Peder said.

"Chopping potatoes? They are a bit knobby and sprouting hairs. Don't they remind you of an old lady's chin? Not that I'd eat old-lady-chin soup—"

"Not chopping potatoes. War."

"I know," Miri said quietly.

Peder put down his knife. "We were going home at

last. We were going to get betrothed, and you would teach and record Mount Eskel's history, and I would carve stone . . ."

"We will."

Peder held her fingers. She leaned over the small wood table and kissed him. The sea heaved beneath them, the footsteps of Storan soldiers creaked on deck above their heads, but for a moment, she was not afraid.

They heard movement outside the door and pulled away.

Astrid walked in, pulling at the neck of her dress. "I feel like I can't breathe."

"Go back up top." Miri walked Astrid out of the galley. "You're not used to tight spaces."

"The Storans stare at me, examining the princess," Astrid whispered. "I don't like being watched all the time to see if I'm sitting right or curtsying right." She stopped at the base of the ladder, looking up but not climbing. "I don't want to marry some ancient warmonger to save a kingdom I don't know or care about. I want a boy who looks at me the way Peder looks at you."

"What do you think we should do?" Miri asked.

"Run away," Astrid said in a hush. "But I know enough history now to imagine what's happening out there.

Kingdoms play games, and the people in between get trampled under their boots. I'll do what I can."

"You are able to do more than most," Miri whispered back.

"Because I was born an unwanted cousin to the king of Danland?" Astrid raised one eyebrow. "Or because I'm Princess Helka Appaluna?"

Miri had an impulse to hug her. Astrid seemed startled at first, but then she put her arms around her, and Miri felt Astrid's back tense as if she were holding back a sob.

"It's a lot," Miri whispered, rubbing her back. "Leaving home and pretending and going into who knows what. Even though I'm just an unimposing tutor, I want you to know that I think you're doing really well."

"Is that what you were trying to be, that first day you came into our house?" Astrid asked with a smile, pulling back. "Imposing?"

Miri nodded solemnly. "Ah yes, I was a grave, impressive, fear-inspiring tutor . . . till I fainted on your floor."

Miri helped Astrid back up the ladder and joined Felissa and Sus at a railing. The girls were shielding their eyes with their hands and staring ahead. For three days the only sights had been the churning ocean and the huge Storan warship. But now, land.

"Asland," Miri whispered.

"Are those . . . cliffs?" Felissa asked.

"They're buildings along the harbor," said Miri. "Asland has thousands of buildings."

"Thousands . . . ," Astrid whispered.

"Where's the Queen's Castle?" asked Sus. Ever since learning about the university, Sus was fascinated with the idea of a huge building where people went just to read and learn.

"On a river island up from the bay," said Miri. "It was the original royal palace in Asland—"

"Till King Jorgan built a linder palace in the center of the city. I remember," said Sus.

They had decided: once in Asland, the girls and Peder would try to escape from the Storans and take refuge in the Queen's Castle. Miri had friends there among the tutors and scholars, and the building itself was a fortress.

"How soon until I can put my feet on solid ground?" Astrid asked the Storan soldiers in her not-that-I-care princess voice.

"Within the hour, Your Highness," said the lead soldier. "His Majesty the king will be pleased to hear of your arrival. I understand he has been wishing for family near."

King Fader was in Asland? Peder had just come up on deck, and Miri turned her back to the captain to look at Peder with wide eyes. King Fader would know in an instant that Princess Helka Appaluna was a fraud.

"Oh. Of course," said Astrid. "And when will I see him?"

"We will take you to him as soon as we dock," said the soldier. "The king has taken up residence in a fortification the Danlandians call the Queen's Castle."

"Very well, that is all," Astrid said, so the soldier would walk away.

Miri felt sick, as if her stomach were not yet used to the swell of the ocean.

She whispered, "Peder, can you swim?"

Fear entered his eyes as he seemed to realize what she had in mind.

"I learned in Lesser Alva," said Miri. "But—"

"I can do it," he said quickly.

She put her fists on her hips and looked at him hard. The only water in the village of Mount Eskel had been a snowmelt stream. They drank from it, sometimes bathed in it, and occasionally pushed each other into it. But it was not deep and much too cold to spend time swimming.

"I will not let you drown, Peder Doterson, just because you pretended you could swim."

"I meant, I could try," he said.

"They won't expect us to jump into the water," Sus said. "It *is* our best chance."

They whispered the plan to one another, over and over. Miri gripped her skirt with her hands, fearing the soldiers would see them shaking. Peder kept clearing his throat.

"Did you say something?" asked a soldier passing by.

"Hm? Oh, nothing," said Peder. In his nervousness, his voice sounded much higher.

Miri did not want to tell Captain Bodel. "I don't completely trust him. What if he decides to betray us?"

"I owe him," Peder whispered.

He went to the captain and spoke low in his ear. Captain Bodel showed no expression, only nodding.

They waited until the ship's sails lowered and rowers brought it closer to the docks of Asland harbor. The tide was low, and beneath the docks, the pilings holding them up rose like a bare winter forest.

Miri handed Peder a small, empty barrel. It was watertight, its lid nailed on. He gripped it with both arms.

"Strike swiftly," Astrid said.

"Aim true," Felissa and Sus replied.

Astrid nodded. The five of them kicked off their shoes, clambered onto the railing, and leaped over the side.

Even though it was a small ship, the gray ocean seemed miles below. As she fell, Miri's body tensed for what would come next—cold water, jarring impact, or perhaps the unexpected sting of a musket ball. In midair she and Peder met eyes. His looked as gray as the sea.

Chapter Twenty

The cargo in the hold
Is as heavy as the sea
The cargo in the hold
Could pull this ship right down

Your love in my heart
Is as heavy as the world
Your love in my heart
Will pull this man right down

They jumped!" Miri heard one of the Storans shout as the water rushed at her.

The splash felt like a punch. Swimming in warm swampy inlets had not prepared her for the brutal, briny cold. She could not force her eyes open, twisting and flailing in the underwater darkness.

Peder! she thought, and vigor sparked in her chest, burning through her limbs. She fought the water, unsure if she was moving up or down. Her lungs wanted air, and she panicked, clawing and kicking, needing to scream so badly her whole body hurt—

Hands grabbed her. The surface of the water broke. Miri gasped.

Felissa had pulled her up. Sus was diligently heading toward the dock. Nearby Astrid gave Peder a push. One arm over the barrel, he paddled with the other, kicking awkwardly against the water.

"Swim!" Astrid said.

Miri swam. The sisters were quick, soon clinging to the log pilings in the shadow of the dock. Miri stayed beside Peder.

"There they are!" Captain Bodel announced from the bow, pointing at the water.

The dozen Storan soldiers were leaning against the railing when Captain Bodel and a few of his sailors grabbed their ankles and tossed them overboard. The vessel rocked to the side, turned, and with full sails headed out of the harbor.

The harbor was full of Storan warships, but their sails were down. Perhaps by the time the warships were in pursuit, Captain Bodel's ship would be away, but Miri did not have the energy to watch for their escape.

Rowboats lowered from the great Storan ship. One went to rescue the floundering soldiers, but another, packed with armed soldiers, began to chase Miri, Peder, and the sisters. With a few swift strokes it would be upon them.

If she did not swim faster, Miri would be caught. Peder breathed in panicked gasps beside her.

"Please," she said, the waves lapping against her face. "Please, Peder, swim."

She heard splashes as the boat rowed nearer. It was almost upon them.

There were hollers from the boat. Miri was so intent on swimming forward and keeping hold of Peder that she did not dare look back.

When Miri and Peder reached the nearest piling, only Sus was there. Felissa and Astrid came up behind them, each swimming with an oar.

"I told Felissa and Astrid to dive under the boat and pull the oars out of their hands," said Sus. "They're stronger swimmers than I am."

Sus smiled as if she was having a wonderful time.

They clung to the pilings while Peder and Miri tried to catch their breath. Her lungs burned, each inhale stabbing her throat. The rowboat drifted not far off, the soldiers aboard hollering at them, yelling for aid from the ship. Another dingy full of sailors began to lower from the warship.

Musket shots. The girls and Peder ducked behind the pilings and began to climb.

Barnacles that were stuck to the crisscrossing logs cut Miri's hands and bare feet. She was the slowest climber, just behind Sus. The world below the dock was as dark as a dense forest, and the wood smelled half-rotted and unfriendly. Water splashed far below.

Astrid was the first to clamber onto the dock. When Miri reached the edge, Peder helped her out and up onto the wooden planks. They did not stop to rest this time but took off at a run. They heard shouting behind them and the clatter of booted feet. One mounted Storan on a fast horse could easily catch them. Miri prayed the Storans had no mounts handy.

Peder knew the streets of Asland better than Miri, and he led the way past the colorful rows of town houses and into the dark, narrow alleys. Footsteps seemed to pursue them, though Miri was unsure if she was hearing followers or just the echoes of their own feet. She saw no carriages or carts, the usually busy Aslandian streets unnaturally quiet. In the distance, three musket pops echoed.

Peder led them down a tight space between two buildings into a small courtyard. A stout man with a shiny head and thick arms was working on a block of stone with chisel and hammer. Miri recognized Gus, the master stone carver who had apprenticed Peder the past year.

He stared at them—four girls and Peder, all wet, shivering, small cuts bleeding on their hands and feet.

"I don't want to get you in trouble, Gus," said Peder. "We'll only stay till it gets dark. Please."

Gus hesitated, glancing at the entrance as if expecting Storan soldiers. But he gestured them into a shed, and they lay flat while he buried them under a huge pile of straw.

Miri's throat was dry, her whole body craving water, and she spent the first hour just trying not to cough. Her heartbeats clattered in her chest, and her ears strained for every city noise. Her own breathing sounded so loud she was afraid their pursuers could hear it from the street.

Hours later, it seemed, she managed to doze, drifting in and out of consciousness, then woke fully alert to the sound of a whisper. It was Peder.

"Let's go," he said.

They all rose, shaking off straw. The sky was solidly black, the city quiet. Her clothes were dry now but her skin itched with goose bumps in the chilly spring night. Peder whispered a farewell to Gus.

"Where now?" Miri asked. "We'd have to pass through the Storan army's camp to get to the palace."

They stood in the narrow alley between buildings, listening for any Storan patrols before emerging.

"They're blockading the palace against the Danlandian army," said Peder, "but a small group might have a chance to slip by. There are holes a rat can crawl through."

"And we're just a bunch of swamp rats," said Sus. "I bet their attention will be on people coming out of the palace. People trying to get in would have a better chance."

"Especially using the route we'll take," said Peder. "A hidden entrance that, um, well, Timon told me about."

"What?" Miri breathed. "How did he—"

"Last year he and his revolutionary-hungry cohorts had made friends with palace workers and learned about the passage. It is too slow and dangerous to move more than a few people through, so they couldn't use it for a full-scale invasion, but as a secret entrance for a few like us . . ."

They traveled in two groups: Peder, Felissa, and Astrid first, then Miri and Sus a block behind. Storan soldiers might be hunting for five people, and they did not want to make it any easier to be found.

Dogs barked, the skinny moon peeked over a rooftop, and a chilly breeze slid down Miri's neck. Gus had warned them that the Storans had declared a curfew. Anyone seen out after dark would be shot on sight. Every sound—every dog bark and click of wind and rustle of trees—seemed to be the footfall of a soldier just about to round the corner.

"I like this," Sus whispered.

"No you don't, Sus. We're in trouble—"

"Not the running," said Sus. "The place. All these buildings. And people are inside, and they all have histories. It's like the buildings are books and if I opened them, I'd learn new things."

The two groups skirted wide both The Green and Commoner Park, where the Storan army camped, and met up again far from the palace. It was now long past midnight.

The sky was cloudy, and a burst of light rain fell like mist. They scrambled down a weedy ravine and plopped feetfirst into a thin stream of stinking water.

Astrid wrinkled her nose. "I don't want to know what I'm walking in."

"No," Peder agreed, "you don't."

They crept on till they found the source of the dirty stream: a metal grate built into the outer palace wall. Palace wastewater was dumped down chutes that traveled beneath the palace, emerging into that gutter. Royal guards should be atop the palace wall watching such grates, but Miri saw none. With the massive Storan army surrounding the palace, the royal guards must have positioned themselves out of musket range.

Peder worked the grate open with tools he'd borrowed from Gus. The rusted metal squeaked like an injured animal, and Miri shuddered, expecting every moment for soldiers to hear and come running.

On hands and knees they crawled in.

The tunnel was completely dark and so low the top scraped Miri's back. The water sloshed around her wrists and knees. Suddenly, it rose to her hips and shoulders, and she tilted her head up, breathing in panicked gasps, her chin wet. If the water gushed higher, there would not be time to crawl back to the entrance. They would be trapped. They would drown. They would—

Miri's heart beat with painful thuds. She took deep breaths, pretending the smell was just the swamp, fierce and alive under a hot sun.

And she thought of home. And wrote letters to her sister in her head.

Dear Marda,

You would not believe the horrible things I had to do today! Thankfully it was over quickly, and Peder and I are just fine and on our way home . . .

As the water receded to a shallow flow, Miri felt something alive scurry past her in the dark. A rat? Her whole body quivered.

Marda, I saw a rat today and was not afraid at all. You would be so proud of me! In fact, we sat down and shared a cup of tea. I told him he looked smashing in a new hat from Elsby, and he promised to pick up one for me the next time he was there visiting his auntie.

The steady noise of Peder's splashing crawl ahead of her stopped. The air felt different, cooler, had more movement. She kept crawling, and the space above her head opened higher. Peder was able to stand. He lifted a metal grate and climbed out, reaching down to help Miri. She clambered out into a large room. The moment she was free of that awful tunnel, her legs shook violently as if they could no longer ignore the panic. She crumpled onto a tile floor.

Around her she saw Sus, Astrid, and Felissa lie down too. Peder sat against a wall, his knees up, resting his head on his arms. No one spoke.

Deep breaths. No tunnel. No water. Light. Alive.

Sus was the first to stand and look around.

"I found drinking water," she whispered.

They all walked or crawled to the barrel, using a nearby cup to drink deeply. Miri felt a little more real.

"Kind of felt safer in Lesser Alva," said Astrid.

In her year living in the palace, Miri had never been in this room before. It was a small kitchen, perhaps serving a minor wing of the palace. A quick search revealed no food. Since the palace was under siege, all the palace residents must have taken supplies to a central location.

They washed up as best they could and began to creep through the palace.

It felt as large as a city. Surely there were enough food stores to keep the palace residents alive until the Danlandian army could return to Asland. If King Bjorn and Queen Sabet could just hold out till their army returned—

No. Miri rejected the thought. If the army returned first, there would be war in the streets of Asland. The destruction could be as devastating as a civil war. Unless they arranged a peaceful ending first.

As they traveled through the palace, eerily empty, the sun rose outside. Pale blue light reached through the windows, throwing long shadows across the stone floor.

They crossed into the linder section of the palace, and that familiar tingle trickled over Miri's skin, surrounded by the stone of her home. Instead of it being comforting, she felt sick with longing. She began to write a new letter in her mind:

Dear Marda,

I wish I'd never left home . . .

Chapter Twenty-one

~~~~~~~~

If the world looks too big, I'll hold you that much tighter
If the breeze feels too chill, I'll make the fire hotter
If the storm booms too loud, I'll sing to you still louder
I'll always keep you safe, my tiny, precious daughter

Miri called out in quarry-speech as she walked. If Katar were in the palace, her friend from Mount Eskel might hear and let Miri know where Britta and the others were.

"I'll check the refuge room," Peder said, speaking of the chamber where they had hidden from revolutionaries with the royal family the previous year. "If you find them first, quarry-speak and I'll come."

"All right," Miri said, feeling very brave, because all she wanted to do was cling to him and cry. The palace seemed as deserted by the living as that haunted house in the tale. Perhaps the royal family was long gone and the Storan army was laying siege to an abandoned building. In which case, they'd just broken into the most dangerous building in Asland.

Miri checked Britta's room. The hearth was cold. She headed toward Queen Sabet's apartment. Astrid, impatient, hurried ahead to the next open door.

Miri felt a strange tang of sorrow, as if she were barely catching a heartrending ballad sung in a far-off room. The sorrow was not her own, the way someone quarry-speaking to her felt different in her mind than her own thoughts. Could all her time in the linder house have helped her develop linder-wisdom? If so, whose sorrow was she sensing? She looked back to ask if Sus and Felissa felt it too.

Felissa had stopped and was doubled over, clutching at her middle.

"Are you sick?" Miri asked. "What's the matter?"

Felissa did not answer, her breathing tight.

Sus looked down the hall. "Someone is sad . . ."

Felissa covered her face with her hands and wept. The emotion must have been very intense, so much so that even Miri could detect it.

"Sus, stay with Felissa," said Miri.

Miri jogged ahead to see what Astrid had found in the next room.

Queen Sabet was standing in front of a chair, as if the sight of Astrid had brought her to her feet. She clutched her hands. Her mouth was open, her eyes wide, almost terrified. Again Miri detected a faint wave of sorrow rolling away from the queen.

"Your Majesty?" Miri said, but the queen did not tear her eyes away from Astrid. "It's me, Miri. You remember? Miri of Mount Eskel? We've just come from Lesser Alva. I've brought the king's cousins. Where is everyone?"

The queen still took no notice of Miri.

"Your . . . name?" the queen asked.

Astrid spoke her name like a question, her eyes narrowing.

"Astrid," said the queen, nodding. "You look . . . you look healthy. Are you healthy?"

Healthy? Had Queen Sabet's mind cracked under the pressure of the besieged palace? Miri took the queen's arm, speaking her name till she finally broke eye contact with Astrid.

"Queen Sabet, we sneaked into the palace. If we can manage it, then so can the Storans. Where's the king? And Britta and Steffan? We need to get his cousins to safety and make a plan—"

"Cousins?" the queen said. Her gaze returned to Astrid. She blinked. A tear shook from her eyelashes and dropped to her cheek, but she did not seem to notice. "Astrid. You look healthy. And beautiful. So beautiful."

Miri choked. Like Miri's, Astrid's hair was wild and her dress torn and filthy from their swim and escape.

"I know who you are," Astrid said.

"Yes, this is Queen Sabet," said Miri. "We should—"

"The painting," Astrid said, her eyes still on the queen. "Before the heat ruined it. That was your face. Why did we have a painting of your face?"

"I thought—" The queen shrugged, a motion as pathetic as the limp of a shot deer. "I hoped that . . . I don't know. I'm sorry."

She turned as if she would walk away.

"No," Astrid said. A command. And the queen stopped, her back still turned. Astrid's voice hardened. "I *know* who you are."

The queen nodded. "I don't feel hatred yet from you. But I know it's coming. And I can't bear—"

"You threw us away—"

"No, please," the queen turned back.

"You never—"

"I had to pretend to myself that you didn't exist," the queen said with a painfully sad shrug again. "My heart tore in half when I let them take you away. And the half I kept never stopped hurting. But I pretended that was normal. I told myself everyone lives with a throbbing scrap of a heart. Don't they? Do you? But I hope you don't. I hope—"

"You could have visited."

The queen nodded, almost eager. "I did at first. When you were little. You seemed happy. Carefree out there with Elin and the wide world to run in. But I was a stranger to you, and it hurt me so much . . . I stopped coming."

"That was selfish of you."

"Was it?" Queen Sabet asked with absolute sincerity. "But why would you want me? A woman who bears a perfect, perfect little baby and wants her and kisses her head, but lets a chief delegate pull her from her arms and just take her away? What daughter would willingly claim such a . . . such a *thing* as a mother?"

Miri sat down without meaning to. Her head felt light and the room was wobbling. She suspected she had not taken a decent breath in a couple of minutes. Everything seemed tilted and wrong, as if the ceiling had suddenly become the floor.

"Did she love you?" the queen was asking Astrid, her eyes yearning. "Did Elin love you as a mother would?"

Astrid flinched.

"She was a good servant to me," the queen went on. "And she loved babies so. I believed she would love you. Did she?"

Astrid squeezed her eyes shut. When she opened them again, she was all cool indifference. "You had years to ask that question, but this is the first time you bothered."

"I asked it." The queen's voice was barely a whisper. "I asked it every day. Just not out loud."

Miri could not seem to stop shaking her head, as if it would force her thoughts to work. She concentrated on breathing.

"I don't expect you to forgive me," the queen was saying. "I deserve contempt and hatred. I hate myself. From the moment I let them take you, my arms have felt empty. I have been holding emptiness for so many years." Her arms hung at her sides, and she tried to lift them as if she could barely remember the purpose for such limbs.

Astrid looked at the queen for several moments before she said, "Yes. Ma loved us. And we loved her."

"I'm so glad," said the queen. She covered her face with her empty hands and cried.

Astrid watched her cry. Surely she must be feeling the same sorrow that had knocked Felissa to her knees and that even Miri could sense in curdling waves, but Astrid just stood like a stone column.

"I was afraid . . . to love Steffan," said Queen Sabet through sobs. "To hold him. If they could take away my baby girl, just take her, then they could take my son too.

I don't know. How could I bear anything? I don't know, I don't know . . ."

"Stop thinking about yourself," Astrid said. "Stop it!"

The queen choked, trying to control her crying. She held out her hands. "What do you want me to do? What can I do? I can't undo anything . . . I hoped that Miri—she's like a candle that never burns down—and I imagined . . . I could imagine her out there with you, bringing you life. And she has a gift, you see, she makes things better, and—I didn't know how—but I hoped she could, she would make things better, and I . . ."

Her eyes lit up as if with a wonderful thought. She rushed over to a window. "Look! When I was pregnant with you, I had these window seats made. I thought, well, perhaps my child must grow up in a sprawling, unfriendly palace, but at least she'll have window seats to curl up in and watch the rain outside. A place to read a book or just be alone if you liked. See? I added cushions. I picked the yellow myself—it's such a happy color. You could come sit here any time you like. It would . . . it would make me happy to see you here. I know that's not . . . there's nothing that I could . . . I wish sometimes Bjorn had warned me when I was making these cushions. He didn't tell me at the time that . . . that I couldn't keep you. If you were a girl. Not until after you were born. He didn't want worry to harm my pregnancy . . . but of course you weren't the only . . . he couldn't save me from worry for long . . . I couldn't save you . . . and I've never sat in these window seats, never once—"

The queen gasped, her eyes wide. She began shivering, as if fighting sobs that were pushing back, threatening to overtake her. Miri turned to see what she was looking at.

Felissa and Sus had come in from the corridor and stood now in the threshold, holding each other's hands.

"All three of you?" The queen's voice was a squeak. "You look . . . healthy. I . . . I . . . I'm so . . ."

Felissa let go of Sus and walked steadily forward. She lifted her arms and put them around the queen.

The touch seemed to be more than the queen could bear. She sank to her knees, collapsing into violent sobs. Felissa sat on the window seat, the queen's head on her lap, and leaned over her, rubbing her back, shushing her as if soothing a child.

Astrid and Sus watched.

"But . . . what about Ma?" Sus said to Astrid.

"Elin," Astrid replied in a harsh whisper. "She was Elin."

"She was Ma," Sus insisted.

Miri quarry-spoke, sending a memory of the queen's

receiving room through the linder to radiate out to the palace and find Peder. As if in response, a call in quarry-speech entered her.

Miri . . .

Not Peder. A sense of Katar in that familiar vibration behind her eyes, and a memory: Miri and Katar in the king's advising chamber.

The confusion and sadness twisted together inside Miri, snapping at her heart, and as she took a deep breath, something that had been stopped up suddenly released. Rage flooded her limbs.

She ran down the hall, opening the door with her shoulder, letting it slam against the wall. King Bjorn sat at the head of a round table with the chief delegate and several other delegates and advisers. Katar stood with a handful of commoner delegates to the side of the room.

"Miri!" Katar said. "You're—"

"It was Queen Katarina, wasn't it?" Miri shouted to the room. "King Klas's twin, who claimed the throne and started the civil war. Queen Katarina put the fear in you—ugly, blind fear that brought you to this." She glared at King Bjorn. "How could you? How *can* you?"

The king flinched.

"You are not privy to the particulars," said the chief

delegate, rubbing his chin as if making sure his tiny beard stayed oiled to a point. "You are in no position to—"

"She wanted her babies, but you forced her to give them away," Miri interrupted. "Shame on you. SHAME ON YOU!"

Her voice was not loud enough to please her. She picked up an empty vase and flung it at the wall, shattering the glass.

The king did not even flinch. His head bowed, and he mumbled down into his beard. "A girl child was born first—"

"Your Highness!" the chief delegate shouted. Clearly the fact that Astrid was older than Steffan was a secret he'd meant to keep.

The king looked too tired to care as he went on. "Since Katarina, only a man can rule. We couldn't allow the chance that the girl would one day challenge her brother for the throne. We couldn't risk another civil war. The kingdom needs stability."

"The kingdom is *people*, Your Highness. People like a baby girl and people like her mother and people like me. And you. And your ridiculous crew of advisers. You don't even make sense! Queens since Katarina have raised girls in this palace who managed not to start bloody wars—oh! Astrid and Steffan are twins, aren't they?"

No one answered.

"And a girl twin was so frightening that she had to be cast far away and her younger sisters too for good measure? The princesses. They *are* the princesses. I probably should have guessed months ago, but I never knew that people such as you truly existed, like the horrid villains in old tales, willing to destroy whatever they—"

"Enough," said the chief delegate. "We have more important matters—"

"Are you so afraid of a baby girl?" Miri said, leaning toward him across the table. "How about me? Do I terrify you too? Watch out, I wear a dress and don't grow a beard, and if you don't keep me in check, I'll steal all your power!"

One of the ministers laughed. Others glared at him.

"Sorry," he said, pressing the smile out of his mouth. "It's kind of funny when you think about it."

"Leave," said the chief delegate.

Miri straightened. "You *are* afraid of me."

The chief delegate grabbed Miri by her wrist and twisted his hand. "You think we have time to indulge your little tantrum? By the creator god, this palace is under siege! If you won't leave, I'll throw you out."

His hand against her wrist seemed to burn, that pressure spreading through her, anger boiling. She pressed her feet against the linder floor and let out a silent quarry-shout: *No!*

The ground beneath them vibrated. The chief delegate took a step back but did not let go.

Miri could shout again, her quarry-speech ripping through the linder stone, up the wall, cracking the stones in the ceiling, pulling them down over his head. Crushing him beneath the weight of a palace once cut from Mount Eskel.

She'd done that before. Confronted with an assassin who had shot Peder, who tried to kill Britta, Miri's quarry-shout had shaken loose the very stones holding up the palace. At the time, she had not known what would happen, only that she needed to stop him. And she had.

This time, she knew. She would be choosing to crush this man to death. She wanted to do it, and the want made her afraid.

"Miri . . . ," Katar said with warning.

Miri gritted her teeth and said as calmly as she could, "Let go of me."

"Leave her alone," the king said wearily. "I rather think this is something worth shouting about."

The chief delegate's grip squeezed momentarily harder before he released her.

"The queen has met them," Miri said, rubbing her wrist.

"Met whom?" the king asked, but he straightened in his chair, his eyes wide with comprehension.

"They're here," said Miri. "And she's . . . she's weeping like she'll fall apart. Maybe Danland deserves to be torn to pieces by Stora, I don't know. But I do know that even ill and dying, my mother wouldn't have let you take me. And that's the kind of person I want to be, the one who's holding on, fierce, fighting for life. You ripped out your own hearts the first time you stole a baby from her weeping mother's arms. You've been living heartless ever since. I should have noticed before. I don't know how any of you are still left breathing."

Miri left and slammed the door behind her. Maybe they'd throw her in a dungeon for a tirade like that. Just then she did not care.

When the door opened, only Katar came out into the hall.

"Are they throwing me in the dungeon?" Miri asked, pacing, the fire in her burning too hot to stand still.

Katar shrugged. She folded her arms, the usual light in her eyes dim.

"My ma died having me too," she said. "But I don't know if she wanted me or not. My pa never said anything."

"I bet she did," said Miri. "And what if the chief delegate came and took you out of her arms?"

Katar was not listening. "A ma would have been a nice thing to have. Or any parent who loves you something fierce. But that idea always seemed like true love or magic fish—something caught only in tales." Katar was facing the wall, staring at a painting. "I figured out who the princesses were, not till after you left for Lesser Alva. Once I realized I wrote to you, but I didn't yell at anyone. I just thought, well, that's how things go, don't they?"

"But they shouldn't."

"I don't know, Miri. Maybe the princesses were better off in Lesser Alva with a woman they thought was their mother, if she loved them."

"Maybe they were," said Miri. She was still trembling, her body tight, as if retching against the injustice of it all, but she stopped pacing and joined Katar to see what she was staring at.

A painting of a red-haired woman in a heavy gold collar and green brocade gown.

"Queen Radisha," said Katar. "She was always my favorite because we have the same color hair. She was luckier than Queen Sabet. Radisha only bore sons."

Or so the history books record, Miri thought. But the linder house in the swamp carried the memory of twin girls with the same red hair and intense eyes. She shivered. Radisha had married King Klas's son. She would have been the first queen after the civil war. If she birthed daughters—twins even—the reminder of Katarina would have still been fresh. Likely it'd been for her daughters that a chief delegate first ordered a linder house built in Lesser Alva.

"You know, I thought you were here when you weren't," Katar said suddenly.

"What?"

"This winter," said Katar. "Twice I heard you quarry-speak to me. The first time I decided it had been a day-dream. The second time was harder to dismiss. It was as if you were quarry-speaking, 'Hello!' Or at least, the memory it nudged in me was the time we returned from the princess academy and ran into the village and everyone came out running and shouting. It made me certain you were all right, even when we hadn't received letters from you for ages."

"But I only arrived in Asland yesterday," said Miri, "and entered the palace early this morning."

"I know. It was silly, never mind," said Katar. "I'll go find Britta. She'll want to see you."

Katar left. Miri turned back the other way and nearly ran into the queen. Again Miri sensed that faint sorrow, heaving and giddy like a memory of seasickness.

The queen was nearly void of expression. "I don't blame you," the queen said.

"For what?"

"For hating me. I've hated myself for a long time."

Did she hate the queen? Anger and sorrow beat at each other inside Miri till her heart felt bruised. She had to clench her fists to keep from shouting again.

"I know they're a bunch of bullies and ignorant tyrants," said Miri, "but couldn't you have stopped them? If you wanted your daughters, couldn't you have just refused to give them up? And then you stayed away. You stopped caring."

The queen shook her head. "Numbness comes after caring too much."

Miri's voice softened to a hush. "You said I make things better. How am I supposed to fix this?"

"You can't."

The queen continued down the hall, running her hand against the stones as if fearing she would fall over.

Miri leaned against the wall herself and shut her eyes. It took effort to slow the angry beats of her heart and remember how to listen to the linder. She exhaled the struggle and allowed herself to open and flow into the images. So few people had lived in the little linder house, but the palace stone was crowded with memories. Guards and servants and people hurrying, up and down the corridors, up and down. Like a gray shadow in the midst of it all, year after year an image of the queen walked, shimmering in solitude, slow with pain.

Chapter Twenty-two

❦

A castle of defense, a bastion of might
A fort where the wise teach the young to fight
An armory of weapons, sharp as hooks
Are wrapped in leather and shelved as books

Miri was so full of the linder's memories she felt half ghost herself, sad and afraid, wandering down the corridor as if through a tale that ends in tragedy.

She entered the queen's apartment and found the sisters staring at Britta and Steffan.

"Miri!" Britta threw her arms around her. "You're safe! You're here! And you're safe! But how did you get here? I don't care, because you're safe! And here!" Britta pulled back. "But I'm so angry at you! I don't want to forget that."

"I wrote, I promise I did," said Miri.

"No, not for that. I feared you'd try to come after me when you should flee to safety instead, and sure enough, here you are, and now we're both stuck in a besieged palace. You're a very good friend and a very naughty person. And you cut your hair!"

Britta's long, pale hair hung loose as if she had found no reason to do it up. Her white linen dress was wrinkled, and Miri suspected she'd been wearing it for several days. But her cheeks were their usual mottled red and gave her a happy, friendly aspect even in that dark, strange palace.

"So these are the king's cousins," said Britta, turning to the sisters. "We exchanged names but I haven't heard a word about how you all got here."

"It's a very long story," said Miri.

"My mother just left," Steffan said, his gaze lingering on the door. "She seemed upset." The prince, in his dark-blue jacket cut at the waist and knee-high boots, looked even taller than Miri remembered.

"You should go after her, Steffan." Miri was not adept with linder-wisdom, but she thought she'd detected in Queen Sabet the loneliness of someone who does not want to live.

Steffan hesitated as if worried a sudden departure would be impolite, but he nodded.

When he'd gone, Miri said to Astrid. "So, that was your twin brother."

Britta took a step back. Miri grabbed her arm and

led her to a chair, remembering how her own legs wobbled after realizing the truth.

But the sisters kept their feet. Sus seemed stunned.
Felissa was crying so quietly Miri had not noticed before.
Astrid's arms were folded, her back slightly turned.

"Do you think we could go somewhere private?"
Miri asked Britta. The queen had left, but she might
return and perhaps the king too.

Britta led them to a guest bedroom in the interior of
the palace. They sat in a circle on a rug, and Miri told
Britta what she knew. The telling of the story helped Miri
swallow the great, lumpy truth of it all, though it sat
now in her belly like a mass of gristle.

"Steffan didn't know," Britta said, her chin trembling.
"I swear he didn't know. Let me go find him—"

"Just give them a little time," Miri whispered. "I don't
think the girls are ready to meet, uh, any more family
today."

Britta did go out to find Peder and brought him back,
along with food for the group. All day she insisted on
fetching them whatever they needed, as if trying to be
one of the servants they were supposed to have had in
Lesser Alva.

There were three beds in the room, but when night
fell, Astrid, Felissa, and Sus curled up in the same one.
Britta shared Miri's bed, Peder bunking on the third.

And when they woke the next morning, they sat on the floor and kept talking. Sleep had stopped Felissa's tears, but her dry-eyed stare and grim mouth worried Miri.

"They so badly didn't want us they hid us as far away as they could," said Astrid.

"I liked the swamp," said Sus.

"So the joke's on them, right?" Astrid said with a bitter laugh.

"They sent us away for fear that our mere existence could start a war," said Sus.

"And now they want you to stop one," said Peder. "They're not making a lot of sense."

"Are you sure King Fader knows about us?" Astrid asked Britta.

"Yes," said Britta. "After Stora invaded Eris, the chief delegate sent a letter. A reply came indicating that the king would accept such an alliance and wished to meet you three. We heard nothing again from Stora for a few months. In the silence, we got worried, and our army marched to our border with Eris, just in case. And then, Stora suddenly took Asland."

"You're never safe when a king knows your name," Peder muttered.

"Elin was my ma," Felissa said. "She always will be."

Peder began to pace. "The palace is under siege, and no one seems to be doing anything."

"The king is confident they can outlast Stora," said Britta. "We have plenty of supplies, and our army should return to Asland any day."

Astrid stood up. "I'm going to the Queen's Castle to see King Fader. I'll let you know how it goes."

"Like mud you will," said Felissa.

"Just stay here, Felissa," said Astrid. "It'll be better if I meet with him without you two."

Sus and Felissa looked at each other. Felissa nodded. And then they pounced. The force of their leap knocked Astrid against the bed, and then they were a pile of girls, writhing and shoving and kicking.

"Whoa!" said Peder. "Um . . . stop?"

"They do this all the time," said Miri.

Sus was sitting on Astrid's legs, Felissa lying across her back.

"Say it!" said Felissa.

"You won," came Astrid's muffled voice.

They let her up.

"We all go together," said Felissa. "If we can end a war, then we should."

"It *is* logical," said Sus.

"I'm going too," said Miri. "I *am* your tutor."

Peder started for the door. "I'll go talk to someone about getting us an armed escort—"

"No," Miri and Britta said at once.

Peder groaned as if expecting what was coming.

"No boys," said Miri. "They're only scared of girls when we're in a crown on a throne. On a battlefield, they mind us no more than dandelion fluff. But as soon as a boy of warrior age appears, they'll load muskets."

"But I'll go with you," said Britta.

Astrid shook her head.

"Please?" said Britta. "Your—uh, the queen is in no shape to go, and they might shoot King Bjorn or Steffan. But after all this, you should have some family to stand by you."

"You're not what I expected when I thought of a princess," said Astrid.

"I still don't feel like one. At the princess academy on Mount Eskel, we all agreed that Miri was more princess than anyone."

"Oh stop it," said Miri.

"Well, at the very least, I've learned how to look like a princess," Britta said. "And since that's what matters most for some, we can play that game."

Britta took them to her own room, where they bathed. Britta combed their hair, working out each snarl delicately, as if she were crocheting lace. They dried by the fire, their locks wrapped around wooden spools to create curls. Britta pinned up Astrid's hair, as befitting her status as a girl come of age and the eldest daughter.

Britta selected dresses for the girls from her wardrobe, choosing colors she thought best complemented their skin tones. Really clean for the first time in months, Miri felt a fresh, cool hope.

When Britta left to explain the plan to the king and his advisers, Miri asked the sisters, "Are you sure?"

"Remember Princess Starla in that story you told us—how she strapped herself to the figurehead of her husband's ship and the enemy didn't fire on it for fear of hurting a lady so brave?" Felissa sighed, though there was more pain than smile in it. "That's a beautiful story."

"A royal marriage alliance *is* more practical than a war," said Sus.

Astrid set her jaw. "What else would we do anyway? Our ma is dead. We can't go back home. This is the only way forward."

Miri understood the part Astrid did not speak aloud—marrying King Fader was the surest way of protecting her sisters.

After a tap at the door, Peder wobbled in wearing one of Britta's fancy pink silk gowns. He could only get the sleeves up his forearms, and his chest was too broad to button up the back. He'd wrapped his head in a lace scarf and was holding a fan shyly in front of his face.

"I'm ready," he said.

Felissa smiled her first real smile since arriving. And then she laughed so hard she was seized with hiccups.

"Peder Doterson," Miri began.

"Come on, Miri," said Peder. "I can't just let you all walk into the enemy camp alone."

"And you can't come with us wearing—or rather, half wearing—that outfit," said Miri. "For one thing, pink is not your color. It completely washes you out."

Peder gasped, mock-offended, and Miri tried very hard to keep a straight face.

Britta came back in, looked at Peder, looked at Miri as if for help, and back at Peder again.

"Hello, I'm Princess Helka Appaluna, your escort to go see King Fader," he said in a squeaky voice.

"He sounds and looks exactly like a girl," said Miri. "The armies of Stora will be easily fooled!"

Peder took off the lace scarf and hobbled forward, the waist of the skirt tight around his thighs.

"Please?" he said.

"What if they shot you?" said Miri. "Armies do that sort of thing."

They argued for a few minutes, eventually changing to quarry-speak until Miri won the debate by sharing the memory of the time an assassin shot Peder. And with the memory rode her grief and fear and pleading.

Peder nodded, letting his fan drop to the floor.

"I'll stay with these three royals," said Miri, "and you stay with the other three. Maybe an ounce of Mount Eskel sense will keep them all alive long enough for Danland's revolution to survive."

Peder kissed Miri, and this time she lingered, so if anything happened, she would not mourn the lost moment.

At the door from the palace to the courtyard, Queen Sabet waited, her hands clutched before her, her eyes down.

Astrid passed by without a glance. Felissa reached out and touched the woman's hands. Sus stopped.

"What's my whole name?" Sus asked.

"Susanna Apollonia Bjorndaughter," the queen said slowly, tasting each syllable.

"When we get back, I have a lot more questions to ask you," said Sus.

The Danlandian palace guards stood in a line near the palace. Across the street in Commoner Park, Miri could see an ocean of Storan soldiers, muskets in their hands. She guessed that the space between the royal guards and front line of the Storan army was a little more than the length of a musket shot.

Miri took a deep breath. "Ready?"

The girls nodded.

Britta led the way across the courtyard. When they passed the royal guard and entered musket range, Miri's muscles tensed.

"You're my ladies," Britta whispered. "We don't reveal your true identities to any but King Fader himself."

"A wise plan," said Sus.

The palace wall was stone and as high as three men. The girls stopped at the cast iron gates. Through the bars, the army of Stora looked back, so many helmets there appeared to be an iron sea. Britta cleared her throat.

"I am Princess Britta of Mount Eskel, wife of Crown Prince Steffan Sabetson," she called out.

A soldier in the front line took one step forward. He wore the high-peaked helmet and fringed sword hilt designating him as more than a common soldier. Like all Storan soldiers, his hair was blond, but so was his beard, so perhaps his head hair had not needed dyeing to achieve the Storans' preferred color.

"I am Commander Mongus," the soldier shouted back. "What can I do for you?"

"I wish to meet with His Highness, King Fader. I expect you will escort me and my ladies with courtesy and safety."

"Sure, I'll take you to King Fader," said Commander Mongus. Something in his tone gave Miri pause. She wished they were surrounded by linder and Felissa could read his emotions.

A royal guard unlocked the gate for them, relocking it behind their backs. The girls crossed the deserted street and entered Commoner Park. The moment their feet stepped on the grass, Storan soldiers with muskets surrounded them. Miri's legs ran with cold fear. Commander Mongus gestured them into a carriage and climbed in after them.

The eyes of the Storan army watched them through the window as they pulled away, with dozens of helmeted soldiers on horseback escorting them.

Miri saw no other carriages or horses on the streets. Some Aslandians were on foot as if trying to go about their normal business but looked startled when the carriage rumbled by. The entire city trembled with fear.

When the carriage turned a corner toward the Queen's Castle bridge, the silence broke. Miri pressed against the window, eyeing a mob of Aslandians swarming around them, assaulting the carriage with shouts.

"Stora, go home!" she heard the Aslandians yell.

The Storan soldiers on horseback pointed muskets at the crowd, and the crowd screamed and dispersed. Miri had not recognized any faces, but she wagered some of the people who were now standing up to Stora were the same who the year before wanted a revolution and the death of Danland's King Bjorn.

Commander Mongus did not even bother to glance out the window but just leaned back against the seat.

"They are dogs without teeth. Believe me, if they did bite, we would slaughter the lot."

Britta stiffened. "Danland is not small and weak, no matter that you disabled Asland's harbor. It would be foolish to believe you could hold Danland as easily as you conquered Eris. When our army returns—"

"We will be long gone. We've simply come to kill your king."

Miri gaped. "What?"

"Your king is a liar," said Commander Mongus, "and he dishonored our monarch with his lies. Stora cannot allow southern scum to degrade the name of our king."

"So, what, you're just going to execute King Bjorn and then leave?" said Miri.

"Well, maybe we'll take a few treasures home with us. Now that we have that lovely harbor in Eris, we wouldn't mind your ships to fill it. In the name of honor."

He smiled a cold mock of a smile, perhaps to make them cringe.

Britta did not blink. "You won't breach the palace before the army returns."

"Won't we? Fortunate for you that you escaped when you did. No one in that building is safe for long."

Britta blanched.

The commander leaned closer to Britta, his fake smile a grimace. "Do not besmirch the honor of Stora. The north men defend honor with iron."

Miri's stomach felt cold and sick, as if she'd swallowed the briny sea. He would not tell them so much if he believed they might ever return to the palace to report it to the king.

"You claim to fight for honor," Miri said, willing her voice to sound brave, "but you're just a bunch of thieving bandits."

Commander Mongus held back the tip of his forefinger with his thumb and lifted his hand to her face. She frowned, unsure what he was about. When his hand was close to her nose, he flicked his finger hard, as if knocking away a fly.

"It's dishonorable to hit a lady," he said. He flicked her again and laughed.

Miri's nose stung. She sat very still.

The carriage crossed the bridge to the river island. Outside the window, the Queen's Castle rose, its towers roofed in green copper. The first time Miri had seen the great red-brick structure, she'd trembled with excitement and anticipation. Now her feet felt so cold she might have been standing in a snowmelt stream. It had been easier to feel brave back in Britta's room.

The Queen's Castle was as crowded and busy as the royal palace had been silent. Soldiers camped around it, every window bore a guard. Inside, instead of scholars in robes hurrying to classes, soldiers stood at attention, as still as death.

"It's so big!" said Sus, looking up where the central staircase climbed twelve stories. "I definitely should become a scholar here."

Britta clutched Miri's arm. "Steffan . . . ," she whispered.

"That Commander Mongoose is a liar," Miri whispered back. "Steffan is safe."

Britta nodded, wanting to believe that was true, just as Miri wanted to believe that Peder was safe too, and that the Queen's Castle would be a university again, and that Dogface would have Lesser Alva back, and that she would be home soon, running into her pa's arms, falling into her sister's embrace.

Commander Mongus led them into a large room, thinly lit by narrow windows. It had been the master tutor room. Gone were the bookcases and tables where white-haired tutors pored over ancient parchments. Now the room was busy with soldiers poring over maps and lists of supplies.

"Tell High Commander Paldus we have a royal visitor," Commander Mongus told another soldier, who bowed and left.

"We're here to see King Fader, not your high commander," said Britta.

"That's not possible," said Commander Mongus. "But High Commander Paldus is authorized to make all decisions on behalf of Stora's honored king."

"We came on good terms, putting ourselves willingly into Storan hands for that purpose alone," said Britta. "My ladies and I have earned the right to meet with your king."

"In matters of war, Princess," said Commander Mongus, "fighting, not surrendering, gains you respect."

"In that case," Astrid said, speaking up for the first time, "I'll fight you."

Miri had no doubt she meant it.

Chapter Twenty-three

Brave men of the north be blessed
Leave your wife and lock the door
Gone is peace, no time for rest
Howl with rage and run to war
Beat your shield and beat your chest
Raise your sword and raise a roar
Life is quickened in your breast
Battle is what life is for

Astrid was dressed in pink silk, her hair curled, her posture so straight she could probably balance a boot on her head while at a dead run. She looked like the potential bride of a king, but her hands were in fists, lifted and ready to punch.

"Pardon me?" asked Commander Mongus.

"I will fight you," she said again. She kicked off her slippers and tied the back and front of her skirt together, the knot between her knees to allow her more movement.

Commander Mongus smiled with a corner of his

mouth. "Perhaps you should wait downstairs until the high commander decides what to do with you." He turned his back to Astrid and began to speak with another soldier.

Before it was a university, the Queen's Castle was just that—a castle. Miri knew that downstairs were the old dungeons. They were about to become prisoners of war.

"A champion match," Sus whispered.

"Yes!" Astrid strode forward. "I challenge one of you to a champion match. If I win, then we earn an audience with King Fader."

The soldiers laughed.

"Are you laughing at a lady?" said Astrid in her Princess Helka voice. "That would be extremely uncivil."

"Astrid, are you sure?" Miri whispered.

"What do we have to lose?" Astrid whispered back. "Besides, I really want to hit someone."

Commander Mongus was frowning. "Champion matches are no longer respected under—"

"Stora's own King Michel respected the results of a champion match not one hundred years ago," said Sus. "Surely *you* respect your own honored history."

Miri had a vague memory of that detail from the book on Stora.

"Storan soldiers do not fight girls," said the commander.

"Afraid you'll lose?" said Astrid.

The soldiers laughed again.

"Choose a man to fight my sister," said Sus. "Using no weapons but your own bodies, the victor must bring the loser into clear submission. Your champion should beat my sister handily. And when you do, the laws of a champion match state that, as the instigator, her life will be forfeit."

Miri sputtered. What was Sus saying? Astrid would be executed *when* she lost?

"Wait—" Miri started.

"Let her try," Felissa whispered. "She's wrestled more than one caiman."

But a caiman lived in water. And in the swamp Astrid had sharp sticks and caiman poles and sisters. In Miri's experience, there was no predator more dangerous than a man.

The commander still would not look at Astrid. He addressed Britta. "The north men do not wrestle lady's maids. I don't have time—"

"I am not a lady's maid!" said Astrid. "I am Princess Astrid, daughter of Their Royal Highnesses, King Bjorn and Queen Sabet of Danland, and I demand a champion match."

Commander Mongus walked up to Astrid, so close

he breathed on her face, and he poked her collarbone with his finger. "You are a liar," he said in a low growl.

"Keep insulting me," said Astrid. "Makes me want to fight you even more."

The commander's face was deathly still. "Very well, you deserve this. Sten?"

Sten was half a head taller than any other soldier in the room. And he was wide. And bore visible scars on his hands. He looked to Miri to be the kind of man who would not mind hitting a girl.

Sten unbuckled his sword belt and handed it to another soldier.

"Strike swiftly," Felissa whispered.

"Aim true," said Sus.

Sten started to turn toward Astrid, but Astrid did not wait. She took one, two, three running steps and jumped, ramming her head into his belly and knocking him to the floor.

It took a few moments before he managed to suck in a breath. He started to flip over onto his hands and knees. Miri wondered if Astrid not only expected this but hoped for it. After all, the safest way to wrestle a caiman was from behind. Astrid sprang, kneeling on the back of his neck to push him back down. She slid her right arm under his neck, locking her right hand onto her left arm and pushing his head down with her left hand.

Instead of standing, he tried to reach around and grab her. She ducked her head and clung on. A caiman would take its prey underwater, Miri remembered, and hold it there till it could no longer breathe.

Take his breath! Miri wanted to shout.

Sten pushed against the floor to stand, and still Astrid clung. His face was turned a deep red. He grabbed her shoulders and flung her off his back. She tumbled and kept rolling to get some distance between them. Sten wobbled for just a moment but seemed to recover. Standing, he was nothing like a caiman. He punched at Astrid, and she ducked. He punched again, and she managed to roll to the side. If just one punch from that large fist connected with her head, the fight would be over. And perhaps Astrid's life.

But the third time he punched, she ducked low and came up again with her head hard into his gut right below his lungs. He staggered and fell on his backside.

This time he stood up fast. But perhaps too fast because he froze, blinking rapidly, the lack of breath and blood to his head finally catching up with him. He stared, as if trying to follow the path of a dust mote in a stream of light. His eyelids twitched, and then his legs buckled and his whole body hit the floor.

Astrid leaped onto his back and pulled her fist back, ready to strike his head.

"I'd rather not kill him," she said to the commander. "Say I've won and I'll stop now."

The soldiers just stared, some shaking their heads as if trying to make sense of what they'd just seen.

"Say it!" said Astrid.

"You won," said Commander Mongus, surprised by his own words.

Other soldiers leaned over Sten, checking him for injuries. His eyes were closed, but he began moaning.

Astrid crouched beside him. "Are you all right?"

"Ow," he said thickly.

"You fainted," she said.

"Ow," he said again.

He sat up, woozy, his hands to his head. Then he glared and pointed at the soldiers circling around him. "I'll kill the first of you who dares taunt me."

Felissa and Sus hugged Astrid.

"We've got meat," Astrid whispered.

Britta took Miri's hand, and Miri squeezed back.

The door opened, and several men entered, led by one who was as tall as Commander Mongus. Miri wondered if Storans chose their leaders by height.

"High Commander," said Commander Mongus with a short bow, the other soldiers in the room offering deeper bows.

High Commander Paldus's head hair was not dyed blond but had turned entirely white with age. He was still tight with muscles, his face only lightly wrinkled. Like other Storan soldiers, he wore gold chains around his neck. His chains glittered with jewels.

"What are these girls doing here?" he asked.

Commander Mongus gestured to Britta. "This one is bride to Prince Steffan and insists on meeting—"

"Put them in the other room," said the high commander.

Soldiers escorted them out of the master tutor room and into a side chamber, keeping an eye on Astrid, as if expecting her to suddenly attack.

They shut the door on the girls and the lock clicked. Miri rolled her eyes. The girls were here on a mission to meet King Fader. They were not likely to try to escape.

The room was much smaller than the previous one. Wood-paneled walls, cream-colored tiles. Though emptied of furniture now, Miri thought she recognized the chamber. There was one other door, also locked. The windows were narrow, as if for archers. Even if she broke the glass she could not fit through.

Miri stooped to investigate the fireplace. Master Filippus had shown her several novelties in the Queen's Castle, passages that opened beside fireplaces, hidden closets, secrets built into the castle for long-ago rulers. Miri examined the mantel with her fingers, searching for a hidden lever.

Astrid was pacing. "I don't know what to wish for. I want King Fader to dislike us and send us back home. But then again, I want him to end this war and let everything go back as it was."

"I just hope I get a chance to write about that champion match for the sake of history," said Miri.

Felissa stood at the window, the light outlining each of her curls in gold. An old, proud king seemed likely to choose whichever girl looked prettiest in a dress and curled hair. But would Felissa be able to keep laughing, far away and married to an elderly, belligerent king?

"I'll marry him myself before I'll let him have Felissa," Astrid whispered. There was no linder in this castle, yet Astrid still seemed to guess what Miri was feeling. Miri nodded.

The door from the corridor opened. Miri startled away from her search of the fireplace.

Commander Mongus leaned against the doorjamb. He pulled a knife from the sheath in his belt. The hilt was a creamy white, and Miri thought, *walrus ivory*. She waited for him to speak, but he started trimming his nails with his knife. The sound of it was slick and sharp, the kind of blade that can cut bone.

"Take us to King Fader," said Astrid.

"It's fascinating how long it's taking you to realize that won't happen," said Commander Mongus.

"Astrid won the champion match," said Miri. "And you yourself promised us a visit with King Fader. Did you lie?"

"Certainly not." Commander Mongus touched his fingertip to the point of the knife. "Lies are for cowards and dishonored wretches."

"We earned the right to see him," said Miri. "We've managed to sneak here all the way from the west—"

"The west?" Commander Mongus straightened up from the doorjamb. "Wait . . . who are you girls really?"

"They're my companions," said Britta. "Now let us see King Fader as you promised."

Commander Mongus glared, unknown thoughts ticking behind his eyes. He no longer held the knife casually but gripped the hilt in his fist. "King Fader is dead, may the creator god keep his bones. Are you ready for me to send you to him now?"

Chapter Twenty-four

Linder kinder
Locked in stone
Hammer's clamor
Bares the bone
What's the matter?
No one's home

What Miri wanted right then, more than anything else in the world, was her pa. Tall as a tree, broad as a boulder, her pa with his stone-splitting mallet on his shoulder, and behind him the whole village of Mount Eskel bursting through the doors and facing down this arrogant commander.

Mount Eskel was days away. No linder rested beneath her feet; nothing and no one from her home could hear her quarry-speak or would come to her aid.

Miri did not know what to do. So she opened her mouth and screamed.

She screamed with all the air she had in her. Screamed as if she were a tiny girl hanging from a cliff, calling for rescue. Screamed as if the sound could reach all the way home.

Commander Mongus stepped back. Miri took a deep breath to scream again.

"What is going on?" High Commander Paldus pushed past Commander Mongus.

"He just came in here with a knife and threatened to kill us!" said Miri. "Is that how you treat royal guests? Is that what the honor of Stora is worth? I expected more from you, High Commander. Five unarmed, innocent girls put ourselves willingly into your hands, trusting your sense of honor. But perhaps you have none, fighting under the name of a dead king!"

High Commander Paldus glared at Commander Mongus. He inclined his head, gesturing him out. They left, again locking the door behind them.

"Could it be true? King Fader dead?" Miri returned to probe the fireplace, her fingers rigid with urgency. "Who would be king now?"

"King Fader had over two dozen children," said Britta.

Sus looked up, as if seeing the genealogical chart in her mind. "The eldest was a girl, Madel, then a boy, Unker, both grandparents themselves."

"If Fader is dead . . . then we're not needed anymore, are we?" Astrid said.

Miri detected a little regret hidden in the relief of

her words. Astrid did not want to be forced into anything, but she had not minded being needed.

"Stora will still find a way to use us," said Miri. "If they—*ah-ha!*"

A small decorative panel near the floor pushed back against her fingers, and a larger panel swung open, creating a narrow doorway beside the fireplace.

"Quick!" said Miri. She ushered them all through the opening, entering last and pulling the panel closed behind them.

They were inside a wall, the space so tight Miri had to walk sideways. Dust as thick as mud swirled around her feet, rising up into her hair. She covered her mouth with her sleeve and tried to swallow a cough.

"There's a ladder," Astrid whispered.

Miri gestured that they should climb. She was the last up what were just boards nailed to the inner wall, some pieces so rotted they crumbled under their fingers like old bread. Miri gripped the narrow holds, her legs trembling, her lungs aching to cough.

The ladder spilled them into a second-floor between-walls space, this one a little wider than Miri's shoulders and as long as a man. They huddled there, listening to movement on the other side of the wall.

"What's your plan, Miri?" Britta whispered.

"To hide until I think of one," Miri whispered back.

"Are there more of these passages?" Astrid asked through her sleeve.

"I think they run all through the castle."

Astrid's eyes were watering. "Then let's find one with less dust and danger of sneezing."

Felissa, pinching her nose, nodded in agreement.

So they tiptoed and climbed, tiptoed and climbed, by the light that came in through the cracks. They stepped over piles of things others before them had hidden in the walls—dried up leather, empty bottles, books reduced to scraps by moths. They passed other secret doors that would lead them out, but voices and footsteps always murmured from the other side.

Surely by now the Storans had discovered an empty room where the five girls had been. Would they think to look inside the walls?

They'd climbed up so many nailed ladders Miri expected to emerge into the sky when they stepped out instead into a tiny room. The floor here was not nearly so dusty, and as they stood and breathed, Miri could hear no footsteps through the walls. This far up in the castle, they seemed to be alone. A tiny window bore a glass pane thick with bubbles, offering a distorted view of the gray river under a sky choked with clouds. The island below moved with soldiers, as busy as an ant hill.

"Look," said Britta. She'd found a bundle of a cloak,

with no sign of moth bites or age. Wrapped inside was a flask of water, a stack of cookies, and a set of wooden soldiers. "Someone's been here recently."

Miri shook the flask, discovering it was half full—not enough to last the five of them for even a day. They each took a sip to clear the dust from their throats and talked in urgent whispers, discovering no solutions.

A creak. Miri held her breath. Britta squeezed her hand. A small square of wall opened in.

A boy crawled through and let the small door shut quietly behind him before looking into the room. He startled upright.

He was about the same height as Sus, though a little younger, perhaps eight or nine, with sandy-colored hair that hung to his shoulders. He wore a fine yellow coat and trousers, with a short sword hanging from his belt.

"Please don't scream," Miri whispered.

The boy stiffened. "Of course I won't scream. I'm not scared of five girls. I'm a soldier."

"Don't be ridiculous," said Sus, "you're too young to be a soldier."

"Sus!" said Felissa. "Sorry, she's not as mean as she sounds," Felissa said to the boy, but he ignored her.

"I am not," he replied to Sus. "Stora's boys are warriors born."

"Quoting King Tore, are you?" asked Sus.

The boy blinked. "How did you know? I bet you're the Danlandian girls they're looking for and not even Storan."

"I *read*," she said. "I know about King Tore who *allegedly* led the Storan forces to victory against Eris in 214, when he was just eight years old."

"And I'm *much* older than he was," said the boy.

Sus raised an eyebrow as if she doubted that.

"Are there people out there?" Britta whispered, indicating the door he'd crawled through.

"They have more important things to do than sit in the attic," said the boy.

"What's your name?" Miri asked.

"Kaspar," said the boy. "I'm leader of the greatest army in the continent."

"Yes, we found your army," said Astrid, nodding toward the toys in the corner.

"Hello, Kaspar." Sus curtsied as if practicing a Poise lesson. "I am Susanna Apollonia Bjorndaughter, princess of Danland. These are my sisters and friends. And please don't run to the soldiers and tattle on us."

"Sus," Felissa said with warning, but Astrid had already declared herself a princess too, so it seemed too late to worry about keeping their identities a secret.

"I don't tattle. I'm not a little boy." He pulled out his sword. "And this isn't a toy, obviously. It's a *real* sword."

"Who let you have a real sword and go rushing around stabbing people?"

"I haven't stabbed anyone. *Yet*," he said significantly.

Sus laughed. Without her usual serious expression, she looked as young as she actually was. "So, are you going to stab me?"

"No," he said, trying to be serious but smiling anyway. "But I could if I wanted."

He stepped back and chopped the air, making impressive swooping sounds. Sus's eyes lit up.

"Can I try?" she asked.

He handed her the sword hilt first, and she took it reverently.

"Quietly, Sus," Felissa whispered.

"Princess Susanna Apollonia," Sus corrected, looking over the sword.

"So you *are* the Danlandian prisoners?" Kaspar asked.

"If you tell on us, you'll be a real spoilsport," said Sus.

"You can't escape an island anyway," said Kaspar. "Look, this is how you hold it."

Kaspar showed Sus a parry and thrust move. Sus took the sword and thrust, sticking it into the wood wall. She laughed with delight.

"Shh," said Felissa.

"Now who's stabbing things?" said the boy.

"Oh, I stab things all the time," said Sus, putting her foot on the wall for leverage as she tried to pull out the sword. "You don't need something this long to skin a swamp rat or a frog. But I wouldn't mind having a sword when facing a caiman."

"I don't think caimans are real," the boy said.

"They're real. My sister Astrid is the best caiman hunter in all of Danland, but I'll get better as I get older. When they come swimming at you, all you can see is their eyes and a little ridge of their back. They're as quiet as water, and then suddenly, they *snap!*"

Sus clapped her hands at the boy's face. He leaned back.

"Sus, please, no noise," said Miri.

"No one comes up here," said the boy. "That's why I made it my throne room. I'm the king of Stora."

"Kaspar, do you know of any way off this island unseen?" Britta asked.

"I wouldn't tell you even if I did. Aren't you the enemy?"

"Aren't you the king of Stora?" Felissa said with a teasing smile. "We don't have to be the enemy if you say we're not."

"Well, my father would be angry with me if I harbored his enemies," said Kaspar.

"Anyway, a caiman's jaws are this big"—Sus made a circle with her arms—"and can swallow you whole, but even more dangerous is when the caiman pulls you into a death roll underwater. It's scary work, but when you kill it, you shout to the village, 'We've got meat!' And everyone comes running to have a caiman roast. The meat is white and thick and so good, and you just sit and eat and eat till you want to burst."

The boy smiled. "I want to do that. How soon can we go?"

"There's a war on," Miri said. "There won't be any caiman hunting for some time."

"I wish we could go hunting now," he said, occupied with trying to dislodge the sword from the wall. "Everyone made the war sound fun and I was excited to ride a warship, but it's been nothing but boring talking and sitting around. Still, sometimes war is necessary for the good of a kingdom."

"And sometimes it stinks," said Sus. "Storan soldiers invaded our village. They killed an unarmed man just for getting into his own boat. That's what happens in war. If you'd read *A History of Peace*, you'd know."

"I have read it," said Kaspar.

"Oh?" said Sus. *A History of Peace* was one of the books Miri had tried to explain to Sus from memory. "What did you think about Master Trundell's theory that all progress begins with education, and whenever war begins, education ceases?"

"You know, I overheard someone quote that very bit to Commander Mongus when everyone was talking about invading Eris, but Commander Mongus said that things written on paper and action in the living world have nothing to do with each other."

"That's silly," said Sus.

Kaspar shrugged, still working on the sword. It came loose from the wall and he held it up, grinning. "Someday I'll join the war too."

"Kaspar," said Britta, "is King Fader really dead?"

He nodded, taking a few swipes at the air. "Like this, Princess Susanna. See how I keep my wrist straight?"

"Let me try," said Sus.

"Just a minute," said Kaspar.

"I only got a short turn," she said.

"Kaspar, we're in trouble," said Miri. "I think the soldiers mean to lock us up for a long time and maybe even kill us."

"Oh they won't hurt you," said Kaspar, still swinging, his forehead wrinkled in concentration.

"Well, yes, they might," said Miri.

Felissa stepped closer, smiling kindly. Kaspar lowered

his sword. She bent to her knees, and took his free hand.

"I'm asking your aid, Kaspar," she said. "As a gentleman of Stora, can you help protect us?"

His voice warbled lower as if putting on a grand tone. "Of course, lady, because I *am* a gentleman. But you have nothing to fear. I mean, Mongus is a beast sometimes but 'Storan men are honorable all,'" he said as if quoting someone. "Ooh, I want to show you something. I'll be right back!"

Kaspar sheathed his sword and scampered out the tiny door.

"*Who* is he?" Astrid whispered.

"I'm betting the high commander's son," said Miri. "Only a high-ranking officer could bring family to war."

"Maybe he is a king," said Sus. "After all, I turned out to be a princess."

"King of what?" said Astrid.

"King Fader did have a son named Kaspar, though there are . . ." Sus briefly shut her eyes, as if counting, ". . . twelve others in line for the throne before that Kaspar."

"What if he's going to get the soldiers?" said Britta.

"He won't," said Sus.

"He might," said Astrid. "Miri?"

Miri shook her head, meaning she still had no plan. The day was a game board, and the Storans were well-placed pieces about to win. The only moves for Miri's pieces were to evade and retreat. Except for Kaspar. He did not quite fit, and she thought to wait and see what he might do.

But night slouched outside their tiny window and he still did not return. The girls finished the water. Miri's few slender drops seemed to miss her dry throat altogether.

Astrid stood. "I'm going."

"No, let me," said Miri. "Maybe I can find a path out of the castle now that it's dark, or at least some more water."

Felissa shook her head. "We stay together."

They climbed back into the walls, descending down crumbling ladders, inching through dusty passages, alert for sounds through the walls. They crouched on the other side of one secret door for some time, listening. Between her own anxious breaths, Miri heard nothing but silence. Finally they emerged into a dark storage room packed with furniture. They sidled out of that maze and into an empty corridor.

They were creeping toward a staircase when footsteps resounded behind them. The girls ran. The bootfalls began to chase. Miri turned a corner and slammed into a soldier. And like that, all five girls were caught as easily as flies in honey.

The soldiers marched the girls downstairs, not to see High Commander Paldus but lower and lower still, the weight of the entire castle above, pressing them into darkness. Down where walls were rough cut right into the stone of the island and dungeons still slunk in the deep. The jagged rock glistened with water, and Miri could hear the river roaring as if it were about to break through and pound into the room.

The soldiers deposited the girls into a cell and locked the iron-barred door. The walls were mud-colored bricks, the only light from torches on the cellar wall, flickering through the bars to paint black shadows on their faces.

A voice called out, thick and hollow, from the cell beside theirs. Miri scooted closer to the wall.

"Yes, hello, who's there?" she said.

"Master Hansa," he said.

"I'm Miri Larendaughter of Mount Eskel, and I'm with—"

"Miri? Miss Miri?" A second voice called out, as thin and crinkled as old paper.

"Master Filippus!" she cried back. "Are you all right? What's happened?"

"Stora happened," he said. Miri imagined his eyes crinkling with a smile, the white of his hair and beard gray in the shadows. "They came, we cowered, and they tossed us down here to deal with later. Most of the scholars they let escape across the bridge, but we master tutors are apparently too *dangerous* to let free." His voice warbled with age.

"I don't understand what they're doing," said Miri.

"Well, Miss Miri, I may be a useless cowering old man, but I understand a great deal. I have read dozens of books about Stora, after all."

"They were right, Master Filippus—you *are* dangerous."

So she told him what they knew.

"'The north men defend honor with iron.' The commander said those words?" asked Master Filippus. "Then this might be an honor war. Storans admire their own ethics above all else. If King Bjorn committed a crime against them, they could use it to justify an attack on Danland."

Britta was pressed against the wall close to Miri, listening with her whole face tense.

"If they believe King Bjorn guilty, would Stora justify killing his son as well?"

"Historically, there is precedent," said the master.

Miri could feel Britta shiver. She put an arm around her.

"They're besieging the palace," said Miri. "But they can't think the king will run out of food and surrender before Danland's army returns. It's expected any day."

"Mmm, clever," Master Filippus said. "Small bands of Storan soldiers could make strikes against Danland's army as it travels, slowing it down. Meanwhile, the Storans have impressive stocks of gunpowder. If King Bjorn doesn't surrender, they could make bombs, set them outside the palace walls at night, blow it to bits, invade, and capture all they find within."

The guard's boot steps paced outside their cell door, and Miri fell silent. Britta's shivering turned into crying. Miri held her, and they worried silently together.

Master Filippus was just guessing, of course. But Commander Mongus had hinted that they were already breaching the palace wall in some way that the royal guards did not notice.

No one noticed. The king and his delegates and advisers. The queen, crying in her room, Steffan there, consoling her. Peder and Katar, waiting to see if King Fader would honor his previous promise, wed one of the royal sisters, and form an alliance with Danland that war would not dare to break.

But it seemed King Fader was dead. There was no simple way to end the war. Stora could not hold Danland as easily as it now held Eris, but they would not try. They were here for an honor killing. If the Storans breached the palace wall, the royal family might believe they could surrender and depend on the Storan army's honor to keep them alive while they waited for Danland's army to rescue them. But the Storans were here to kill the king and perhaps the royal family too. And no one in the palace knew.

This winter, twice I heard you quarry-speak to me, Katar had said.

Long nights and empty days Miri had sat alone in the little linder house, in a swamp that had seemed to gnaw on her and try to spit her out. Hours quarry-speaking to the void, believing no one could hear, clutching the hawk Peder had carved.

Was it possible that Katar had heard her all the way from Lesser Alva? One time Miri had managed to send quarry-speech from the princess academy all the way back to the village, a three hours' walk. But then she had been in a building full of linder and on Mount Eskel itself, which was scored with veins of linder where the quarry-speech could travel. Here Miri was surrounded by bricks and ordinary rock.

Miri plucked the stone hawk from her pocket and turned it over in her hands. Its edges were smooth, polished by her frequent touch. This was likely the only piece of linder between her and Peder.

Miri gripped her linder hawk and sent her quarry-speech into it, as if the small stone hawk could grip her silent words and take flight, out of the dungeon, toward the white stone palace. Perhaps distance did not matter so much, just as she did not need to be near Peder to love him.

With her breath alone, she sang a quarry song to focus her thoughts. "Hammer's clamor bares the bone. What's the matter? No one's home." She tapped her foot, the rhythm of quarry work, the beat of her heart, the thumping need in her gut all tied to the hawk in her hands. And silently she sang.

The Storan army.

The king and queen.

The water tunnel.

Image after image, she sang silently into the rock in her hands, repeating the memories that Peder might understand: *crawling through the tunnel, the king, the queen, Steffan. The tunnel, the tunnel . . .*

In the monotony of the task, other words drifted through her mind. Peder saying, "You're never safe when a king knows your name." And Dogface saying, "Fix this." And from Marda and Pa the months of silence and separation, like a great hole in the center of the floor where she might slip and fall in.

She quarry-spoke to Peder. She quarry-spoke to Katar. She hoped one might hear her—or both, and they might say, Yes, I hear her too. That means we're not imagining it. We need to get out.

And Miri clung to the linder hawk, an eye and beak making a perfect indentation in her palm.

Chapter Twenty-five

Close up your ears, child
And shut up your sight
Knock upon your heart
To know what is right

Deep into the night, Miri lay on the floor quarry-speaking while the other girls slept, the linder hawk clutched in her hands, her fingers cold and stiff. In her exhaustion, the activity mingled with the memory of another night when she was held captive, desperate for Peder to hear her quarry-speech. So familiar, as if her self then—on the floor of the princess academy, surrounded by bandits—lay beside her now. Her former self like a ghostly younger sister, the two Miris quarry-speaking together, one on harmony, one on melody.

Then she'd been pleading, *Please, come get us.*

Now she was shouting, *Please, run away.*

Then, she had received a response—a distant call in quarry-speech from Peder letting her know he'd heard.

But now, there was nothing. Perhaps the hawk was too small a piece of linder to collect Peder's replying quarry-speech and echo it back to Miri. Or more likely he simply could not hear her at all.

He can't hear me. The thought became louder than the memory she was singing into the linder. So she shouted at it to go away and kept trying. Fell asleep still trying, curled around the linder hawk, clutching it with both hands.

Miri expected to sit forgotten in the darkness for days, but it was only the afternoon of the next day when their cell door squeaked opened. A guard brought them water to drink and wash their faces and then politely asked them to accompany him upstairs, as if they were honored guests. Though unfed honored guests. Someone's stomach squeaked with hunger.

The morning sunlight stunned Miri's eyes, and she stumbled against the steps leading up to the castle's ground level.

"This was Queen Gertrud's castle," Britta whispered. "You are her descendants. Remember, you are home."

Astrid straightened her shoulders.

Britta took Miri's arm. Felissa, Astrid, and Sus took hands, and connected they entered an enormous room.

Formerly the castle's great hall, the university tutors had used it for group lectures. Now it housed the center of operations for the Storan high commander, leader of the invasion.

High Commander Paldus sat stiffly in a carved wood chair at the head of a long, narrow table. In the morning light that rippled through the windows' thick, ancient glass, his nearly white hair looked silver. Several soldiers stood at attention around the room. Commander Mongus sat at the table, his back to them, but Miri recognized his long blond hair.

"Princess Britta," High Commander Paldus said with a nod.

"High commander," she said with a small curtsy. A very small curtsy.

"Where is the king?" he asked, returning his gaze to the papers on the table before him.

Miri blinked. This was not a question she'd been expecting.

"I have no idea," said Britta. "We came here to meet with him, and then your Commander Mongus there draws his knife and tells us he's dead."

"No, I did not mean our King Fader, rest his bones in the hall of warriors," said High Commander Paldus. "*Your* King Bjorn. Where is he?"

Britta frowned at Miri. Miri shrugged.

"He's in the palace," said Britta. "You know that. You have it surrounded—"

"We have been surrounding an *empty* palace!" said the high commander. "We cracked open its shell last night and found the meat picked clean."

Miri laughed and then tried to cover it with a cough. She put her hand in her pocket and squeezed the linder hawk. Peder had heard. Last night. They'd just made it out in time then. Crawled through the filthy tunnel. Run through the dark streets. Huddled even now, perhaps, under the straw in Gus's shed.

The high commander stood and crossed the room to Britta. "Princess, it's in your best interest to tell me. Where is the king hiding?"

"Honestly, I thought he was in the palace," she said.

"You will tell us where he is, or you will join him on the chopping block when we find him."

"If he's no longer in the palace, then he escaped under your noses," said Miri. "What will you do, burn down every building in Asland? Track down every boat that might have slipped past you in the channel? You may as well search an entire city for one particular rat."

"The best way to catch a rat is with a trap," Commander Mongus muttered, his back still to them.

High Commander Paldus examined Britta's face, scrutinized the other girls, and then leaned against the table to speak close to Commander Mongus. Miri overheard snatches of their urgent whispers.

". . . just get rid of . . . no need of these . . ."

Fix this, Miri thought.

"You start a war of honor," she sputtered, "yet you have none."

Commander Mongus finally turned to look at them. He stood, stalked forward, and slapped Miri with the back of his fist. She fell with the force.

"Do not question the honor of Stora!" Commander Mongus shouted.

"Commander . . ." High Commander Paldus spoke the word as a mild rebuke with no real threat behind it.

Britta helped Miri to her feet. Miri's jaw burned with pain but she kept talking. "You accept an honor challenge, and yet when our champion beats yours—"

"You held a champion match?" the high commander interrupted.

"Hardly, sir," said Commander Mongus. "Sten fought one of the princess's ladies."

"And lost," said Miri. "You were honor-bound to let us speak to your king, but you—"

"No!" said Commander Mongus. "I agreed you could speak to King Fader, and I will happily deliver you to the grave where he resides."

The high commander's eyes narrowed as if he was unhappy with that reasoning, but he did not speak.

"This is the honor of the north men?" Miri said to High Commander Paldus. "Lies and deception—"

"Do not sully our honor," said Commander Mongus. "North men defend honor with iron."

From the corner of her eye, Miri noticed an ornate wood panel in the wall crack open. Was that piece in this dangerous game still in play?

"And I will not have a war of honor sullied by your error," the high commander was telling Mongus.

"It was not a genuine champion match," said Captain Mongus. "The instigator was a girl, a swamp rat, and—"

Miri gasped. "A swamp rat?" These girls were dressed like fine courtiers, nothing to indicate a swamp about them. "You know who they are! But how do you know?"

The commander's expression stiffened, betraying discomfort.

"The soldiers in Lesser Alva didn't know," said Miri, half talking to herself. "So how . . . the letters! You assigned some of your soldiers to travel with the Danlandian traders and get familiar with that part of Danland. They bribed the traders to steal our letters, sending them to you. Katar said she wrote to me about the sisters' real identity. You suspected the truth for some time, and now your suspicions are confirmed. So, why haven't you told the high commander?"

"What is she talking about, Mongus?" asked the high commander.

"Utter nonsense," said Commander Mongus. "I urge you to toss them back in a cell till they're needed to bait our royal trap."

"He kept the secret because the truth of our existence would have prevented the war," said Sus. Her voice was soft and young, yet it cut through all the noise in the room, as sharply as truth. "He's a soldier. He wants war like a farmer wants rain."

"Yes, and this war was supposed to be a war of honor," Miri said, slowly walking closer to the cracked panel in the wall. "But it's based on a lie. King Bjorn offered one of his daughters as a bride to King Fader, and he accepted. After he died, you found out that, at least according to common belief, King Bjorn had no daughters. That was his crime, the reason you justified this invasion—to punish King Bjorn for offering a false princess to a king of Stora. But Commander Mongus found out the princesses were real after all and hidden away in the west, didn't you, commander?"

"Enough," he said.

"Tell your high commander, Mongus," said Miri. "Tell him what the letters said. Who are these girls?"

"I will not be insulted," Commander Mongus said. "I

could have taken you away, had you killed! But I brought you here. I *am* a man of honor, and if you accuse me otherwise again—"

"King Bjorn does have daughters," Miri shouted to the high commander. "Three. And here they are before you. There was no lie—"

This time when Commander Mongus backhanded Miri, he struck her shoulder and sent her slamming into the wall. She heard her collarbone crunch. The colors in the room seemed to vibrate with black and silver, the floor listless, pitching.

Hands were on her—Felissa, Britta, Astrid—but Miri kept perfectly still. Even taking a deep breath sharpened the pain to a dizzying intensity.

Kaspar stepped out of the swinging wall panel, no sword today, his gray wool jacket dusty.

"What is going on?" he said.

"Kaspar! Where are you coming from?" said the high commander.

"That girl said that you would lock her away or kill her, but I said, 'Storan men are honorable all' and now you are hurting her!"

"You should not be talking with the enemy," said the high commander. "Go back to your apartment—"

"No! I promised to protect them."

"I'll get rid of them myself," said Mongus, reaching for Miri.

She whimpered and huddled lower, afraid of his touch. Britta and the sisters stepped between her and Mongus. Miri's heartbeat felt like mallet blows against her breast, finding every crack in every bone and threatening to shake her loose. But she had to keep speaking. She had to fix this. With a groan, she tried to stand.

"Stay down, tutor," Astrid said through clenched teeth.

Felissa faced the commander. "Stop! In the name of the creator god and my buried mother's bones, do not touch her again!"

Commander Mongus flinched.

"You will listen," said Felissa. She smiled, and the smile was kind. "You will do us that much courtesy, won't you? You will stop trying to resolve a problem by beating up a young girl? We just want a conversation. What harm could words do?"

I am their tutor, Miri thought, and though pain shredded her chest, a warmth flowed from her toes up to her crown that felt something like pride and a lot like hope. The warmth cleared her mind, and she whispered to Sus, "I think you're right about Kaspar."

"That's enough, commander," High Commander Paldus said to Mongus. "And Kaspar, you should go at once." He gestured to two soldiers, who took Kaspar's arms.

"I didn't tattle, I swear," Kaspar said to Sus over his shoulder as the soldiers walked him to the door. "I went to get a book and my tutor found me and I couldn't escape again until—"

"Oh!" Sus spoke rapidly, spilling the words out. "King Fader had a lot of daughters but only one son, Unker, who was older than Kaspar. Unker must have died since the book was printed. He had children, but Stora's law is the king's eldest son inherits, so when Fader died, the crown skipped over the daughters and the grandchildren and landed on Kaspar. You are the king of Stora!"

"I told you I was." Kaspar stopped walking, and the soldiers escorting him glanced back at the high commander, hesitant, perhaps, to drag their king.

"They don't treat you like a king," said Sus. "Probably because you're little."

"I am not little!"

"Because you're *young* then. It's not your fault. They're a bunch of dishonorable bullies."

Commander Mongus moved swiftly toward Sus, but Astrid stuck out her foot, tripping the commander. He landed knees-first on the wood floor. The violence jolted the other soldiers, who grabbed Astrid, Felissa, Britta, and Sus, as if afraid they would attack. They left Miri slumped on the floor.

"See?" said Sus. "First he struck Miri, and now he was about to strike me just for making a valid observation. *Bullies.*"

"Kaspar," said the high commander. "I must insist—"

"In Danland not even the head of the army can call the king by his first name," said Astrid. "Shouldn't he call you King Kaspar at least?"

Kaspar frowned at the high commander. "They used to call my father 'Your Grace.'"

The high commander's mouth twitched. "Your Grace—"

"Wait a moment," Sus interrupted, a fist on her hip as she looked at Kaspar. "You're the one who started this war! But that doesn't make sense."

Kaspar's face turned red. "Why, because I'm *little?*"

"No," said Sus, as if she thought that a very stupid question. "Because you seem too smart."

Kaspar scowled at her, trying to figure out the insult.

"Take these girls back downstairs," ordered the high commander.

"Just a conversation," said Felissa again. "Just words."

The soldier holding Sus began to drag her toward the door as she shouted back, "Kaspar, don't let them turn you into another Halffer the Gullible!"

Miri smiled.

Kaspar's eyes widened. "Wait!" he said.

The soldier stopped.

Miri had read the girls the story of Halffer from *The History of Stora*, about a king who let his greedy advisers manipulate him and the kingdom into ruin.

Kaspar scowled. "I'm *not* gullible."

"Maybe the commanders wanted to invade Danland in order to advance their military careers," said Sus, "and when your father died, they decided to use you as a puppet king."

"Don't be ridiculous," said Kaspar.

"It's all right," said Sus. "We only just found out that our mother and father are the king and queen of Danland but sent us away as babies because apparently princesses are too dangerous to have around."

"Oh," said Kaspar. "I'm sorry."

Sus shrugged. "It doesn't matter. I am sorry about your father, though, since you were old enough to remember him and all."

Kaspar shrugged a nearly identical shrug. "I grew up in the country and didn't see him all that often. He was supposed to live to be one hundred. He always swore he would."

"What's his honorific?" Sus asked. Storan kings received honorific titles after their death.

"Fader the Fruitful, because he had so many children," Kaspar said, and then whispered, "It's kind of a boring one."

"Would you prefer something like Kaspar the Bloody?" said Sus. "You don't seem to care if people die or if I lost my home because war is *so* much more exciting than being fruitful."

Kaspar's chin trembled. "War can be beneficial! A passage to the sea is vital for any country, and while we had access to the Northern Sea, sailing around to the channel to trade was dangerous and expensive. Now with the Eris harbor, Stora will thrive!"

Sus opened her mouth as if to argue but then nodded. "Good point. I can see why owning a harbor on the channel would be a vital achievement for your kingdom."

Kaspar blinked, surprised by her turnaround. "Thank you," he said.

"But have you considered Endwil's writings in *Commerce and the Channel Divide?*"

"I've never heard of that book," said Kaspar.

"I bet there's a copy in this castle's library," Sus said.

High Commander Paldus groaned with impatience and ordered the soldiers again to take the girls away. Miri stumbled to her feet before a soldier could yank her there against her will. Her collarbone felt as if it were breaking anew, the pain gagging her. Her forehead was cold with sweat.

Someone needed to do something now or they would be shut up in the dungeon, used as bait to lure King Bjorn and Steffan and Peder out of their hiding place and into an execution.

Please, Miri thought, almost singing it, the thought swinging between quarry-speech and prayer.

Astrid elbowed her soldier in the gut.

Felissa cried out.

Britta said, "Don't do this."

And Sus, her feet dragging beneath her as her soldier half carried her toward the door, announced, "You know, Kaspar, I think we should get married."

Kaspar gaped. Voices of disgust and even amusement boiled around the room. Miri's arms prickled with chills.

Sus hooked her foot around the door frame, and her soldier hesitated, not prepared to wrench this little girl, who was in pleasant conversation with the king.

"Well, I am a princess of Danland," said Sus. "And marrying me makes a lot more sense than killing Danland's royalty and creating unrest in a neighboring kingdom, doesn't it? Especially since there's no longer any honor in this war by Storan standards. Our kingdoms would share resources and knowledge and trade routes, without having to destroy those resources and knowledge and trade routes through war. Before he died, your father did agree to a political marriage with one of us. *He* thought it made sense. Besides, I think you and I would be well matched. I like you."

"Oh," Kaspar said. His face turned red.

"You don't need to be embarrassed by mutual attraction," said Sus. "It's a natural emotion. I've read about it. Or my friend Miri told me about books that talked about it. She's the one your commander was trying to beat up. Anyway, we should be betrothed for now, like Miri and Peder are going to be, and then wait to get married till we're older."

Kaspar just stared.

"Sus," Felissa said. "Maybe Kaspar needs—"

"I don't need to think it over," said Kaspar. "Historically, royal betrothals often happen without the couple even meeting."

"Exactly," said Sus.

"Your Grace," said the high commander. "You don't know what you're—"

"Enough," said Kaspar. "Princess Susanna has made an excellent argument. I think it's more logical and interesting than the war. The outcome will be better for everyone, and then we'll have time to go caiman hunting."

"Good." Sus smiled. "I'm so glad I bumped into you."

"And I'm glad I didn't stab you," he said.

Sus laughed.

"I think she might be really, really smart," Miri said to the girls.

"He's not bad either," Astrid muttered.

"I know what I'd like from you for my wedding gift," said Sus.

"Sus!" Felissa laughed now.

"If my sister is marrying your king," Astrid said to her soldier, "why are you still gripping me like a prisoner?"

"Oh sorry," said Kaspar. "Let her go, all right? And those other girls too."

The soldier with Sus looked at the high commander, who shook his head.

"I am your king!" Kaspar said, his voice straining to be low and thunderous, perhaps in imitation of his father's manner.

The soldiers let go.

"Anyway," said Sus, rubbing her wrists, "I'd like a small house made of linder, like the one my sisters and I had in Lesser Alva. I can sense people's emotions inside linder walls, you know, so it would make a very useful queen's receiving room. Anyway, I bet you'll enjoy bagging a caiman. It's dangerous and exciting—like a war maybe—but much more fun, and ends with meat roasting."

Kaspar's eyes lit up. "We'll go hunting all the time."

"Oh good!" she said. "Before we get married, I'd like to study for a few years and learn as much as I can about being a queen. I don't like making mistakes."

"I didn't tattle," said Kaspar.

"I knew you wouldn't," said Sus. They smiled at each other.

High Commander Paldus crouched to meet Kaspar's eyes. "Your Grace, I'm afraid these girls are tricking you. Let me escort you back to your apartment, and I'll take care of everything."

"Seems to me the two of them have everything already taken care of," said Astrid.

"Yes," said the young king. "Princess Susanna and I have had enough war this year. I'd much rather go caiman hunting. But first I want to show her the library."

"The library!" said Sus.

Kaspar took her hand and they ran off. High Commander Paldus stood up and stared at the door long after they had disappeared. Commander Mongus sat heavily in a chair. His back was to Miri, but this time, his shoulders slumped.

Felissa helped Miri take a seat. Miri breathed hard through her teeth to keep from crying out with the pain. Britta rushed forward, but Miri waved her off.

"I'll be fine. Worry about me later."

Britta nodded and schooled her face. She curtsied again to the high commander, and her smile was kind, nonjudgmental, and open.

"High Commander Paldus, why don't we take a seat and write up the peace treaty? Lady Miri, Princess Astrid, and Princess Felissa will advise me. We should have something to offer King Bjorn by nightfall, and by tomorrow, your men will be on their way back to their homes and families. I'm sure there will be rejoicing all over both our kingdoms."

High Commander Paldus blinked and turned to Britta. He seemed as stunned as a struck fish.

"There was no honor in this war," Britta said kindly. "It is time for an ending."

When the high commander spoke, Miri was expecting a protestation, but instead he said, "I've eaten fresh caiman. Delicious."

Astrid sat beside him at the table and before speaking of the treaty, they exchanged hunting stories. Once or twice, the high commander smiled.

Chapter Twenty-six

We were at once both two and one
My tiny son, my tiny son
Our hearts beat in conversation
Nestled in me like a seed pearl
My tiny girl, my tiny girl
When I spin, you also twirl

Two days later, Miri returned to the palace of stone. Miri had waited until Britta, with advice from Master Filippus, had drawn up an official peace treaty and both King Kaspar and High Commander Paldus had signed it before revealing where Danland's royal family might be hiding.

"Oh, I'm glad *you* knew," said Britta. "I couldn't even guess!"

Sus and Kaspar said farewell for now by engaging in a quick sword fight with broomsticks, and the girls climbed into a carriage. They crossed the bridge and drove to Gus's workshop.

At the sound of Miri's voice, Peder ran out, straw sticking in his curly hair, followed by the king, queen, and Steffan. Gus, the master stone carver—who was now Gus the Royal Stone Carver—exercised his long-neglected face muscles to allow a small expression of relief.

Peder started to embrace Miri but she shook her head. He exclaimed over her arm in a sling. She contented herself by standing near him, laying her head on his shoulder.

"You heard me," Miri muttered against Peder's neck.

"Of course," he said, raising a cautious hand to her back, as if afraid to hurt her. "Though it was kind of sweet how you kept repeating yourself over and over, just in case."

"Miri," said King Bjorn. "When dramatic events happen, you often seem to be around."

He smiled at her, his beard bushing out more.

"It was our pleasure to save your life, Your Highness," she said with a smile.

The king laughed. But the laugh quickly faded when he climbed into the carriage and saw his three daughters. He sat stiffly, his face bright red. The queen seemed to draw into herself, as if trying not to take up any room on the bench.

Miri and Peder squeezed in with the girls, opposite

the king, queen, and prince. Silence rode with them, covered up by the clomp and grate of horse hooves and carriage wheels.

"My, what a lovely day," Miri said with exaggerated brightness, and Peder poked her side.

The army was no longer camped on The Green and Commoner Park, the majority already loading into ships to sail back to the Eris harbor. The Storans had blown four great holes in the palace wall, but the carriage rolled around to the front gate as if that were still the only entrance to the courtyard.

By noon meal, Miri was sitting with the girls in the queen's receiving chamber, a fire in the hearth, a plate of hot, sliced meat and bread on the table before them. She could almost sense the rents in the palace walls outside but the fire lulled her with its familiar crackle and promise of warmth and safety.

The queen sat in a chair in the corner, staring at an open book, though Miri noticed her eyes did not scan the pages.

"It was easier to hate her in the carriage than in the linder palace," Astrid whispered. "I can feel her sadness like it's shooting out of her on steel-tipped arrows."

Felissa nodded.

Miri's subtle skill with linder-wisdom was squashed

by the ache in her jaw and shoulder. She could no longer feel the queen's pain above her own.

"She should have fought harder," Astrid whispered. "She should have visited us. She shouldn't have just given up."

Felissa nodded again. "But—"

The door opened. Miri expected to see Peder or else Katar checking in after the Storans released her with the other palace prisoners. But it was the chief delegate, his small beard pointing into the room.

"Miri Larendaughter, a moment, if you'd be so kind," he said.

She went to the door. He pulled her out and shut it behind her. The suddenness of the action caught her breath, and her mending collarbone shrieked with pain.

"You are a troublemaker," said the chief delegate. He talked close to her face, his eyes wild. "Kingdom shaker, crown breaker. Don't you dare claim victory here. King Bjorn had the daughters, King Bjorn offered one as a bride. Your involvement is meaningless."

"What?" said Miri. "Why are you—"

"I will see to it you do not fool the king into signing over the treasures of Mount Eskel. And I will rid the palace of your contagion. You will not cast doubts on the honest decisions of the past."

"You mean the decision to rip babies from their mother's arms and stow them far away?"

"Other kings before Bjorn have hidden their twin daughters, and no harm done. I will not regret being the first brave enough to say let us rid ourselves of not just any girl twin who carries Katarina's curse but her sisters too—"

"Oh yes," Miri said thickly, "your diligence in keeping the palace free of princesses has saved all of Danland. We should throw you a party. I'll make a cake."

"You dare mock our fear of Katarina the Slaughterer? *You* are her legacy, you who incite revolution and rip the kingdom apart. You are no longer welcome here. Leave the palace and do not try to reenter or you will find yourself under arrest. Go."

"No," said the queen.

Miri had not heard her open the door, but she stood in the threshold now, lit from behind by firelight, the edges of her dark hair a fiery orange. The queen slammed the door behind her, but her long skirt caught it and the door bounced back, still open.

"*You* are dismissed," she said to the chief delegate.

Her eyelids were puffy, her face red, but she stood tall.

"Your Highness," he said with indulgence, as if talking to a child.

"No," said the queen again. "I've had enough of

your speaking to last a lifetime. After Bjorn rid himself of a cankerous official last year, I realized the damage one dark presence can cause. I've read books on law—yes, I *can* read, sir—and the chief delegate's term of office is meant for no more than eight years. You have stayed on much longer because my husband indulges you. He will indulge you no longer. Pack. Leave the palace."

"Your Majesty—" he began again, with far less indulgence.

"The people may elect the delegates from each province, but the chief delegate is the sovereign's to assign. My husband has not always taken my advice but trust that he will obey me on this. You told him to take my babies—" Her voice broke.

"But—"

"Step carefully, sir, or I'll demand you're tried for treason against the crown."

The chief delegate's face was very pale. He looked to Miri and back at the queen. "I was only—"

The queen took a step closer. Her chin quivered but her eyes were hot. "I regret hearing any word you ever said. My body feels made of the stuff, smoldering on regret till I'm nothing but ash. If I have to bear one more of your words I'm likely to burn up."

The chief delegate took a slow, shaking breath.

When he spoke again, it was a whisper. "My lady, you were fine until this girl—"

"I was not fine." The queen's voice cracked. "I haven't been fine for a long time."

The chief delegate's face slowly changed. "I'm sorry," he whispered. "I was afraid . . ."

The queen exhaled, closed her eyes, and Miri suspected she was focusing on the chief delegate's emotions. Miri opened herself to listening not to the memories of the stone but to him. She did not expect to sense anything and so flinched when his emotions rushed easily into her. He was like a huge open sore, bubbling over with the rot of resentment, a jolt of fear, and the ache of regret.

When Queen Sabet spoke again, her voice was soft. "I didn't notice before. You are broken too. You have healing to do. But you will need to do it elsewhere. My girls are home, and I cannot have you here."

The chief delegate covered his eyes with his hand. He took a deep breath. When he faced her again, his face was impassive. He bowed and left.

The queen wiped one hasty tear falling down her cheek. "I am sorry," she said.

"I am too," Miri said. "I was unfair. I wanted you to be the kind of mother who fights for her daughters and wins, but not everyone is a fighter."

"I wish I were."

"Maybe you shouldn't have had to be," said Miri. "But you are. You are now."

When the queen and Miri returned to the room, Astrid, Felissa, and Sus were standing. They had heard through the open door.

"I'm sorry," the queen said again, clutching her hands.

Felissa started forward but looked at Astrid as if for permission. Miri hoped so hard her heart felt floaty that Astrid would run forward and embrace this woman. But when Astrid moved, it was away from the queen. Miri's heart fell heavily into her belly. It was too soon. Astrid could not yet forgive the queen.

But instead of leaving, Astrid walked over to a window. She touched the yellow cushions on the window seat.

"You know, this seems like a wonderful place to sit and read. And pass a rainy day."

She sat on the window seat. She settled into the cushions and opened a book.

The queen exhaled. Something in her softened. Brightened. A small hope alighted on her like a bird on her shoulder.

While Astrid read in the window, Felissa sat beside the queen. And Sus asked questions that the queen tried to answer. When Steffan joined them, Britta and Miri decided to give the family some privacy.

They left, grandly shutting the door behind them, only to stoop beside it, trying to eavesdrop. Giving up, they hurried outside, and standing in a plant bed peered through the window. The afternoon was unfolding around them, flowers in bloom so sweet that Miri wished for a cool drink of water to wash down the scent.

"Look at him," Britta said, shaking her head.

Astrid, Felissa, and Sus sat on one sofa. Steffan sat on another. The crown prince's posture was stiff, his jaw clenched. He gripped a glass of water in one hand and stared at the far wall.

"Oh, he's at it again," said Miri. "He really can do a magnificent impersonation of a stone column."

"He doesn't mean to," Britta said.

"I know," said Miri.

"He gets that way when he's nervous, but they don't know him and will just think he's cold and unhappy and—"

"Look at Felissa," Miri said.

Felissa was smiling, of course. But she kept reaching out, placing a comforting hand on her brother's arm.

"They're in a linder room," said Miri. "They can feel how he's feeling. They'll understand."

"There you are," said Peder.

"*Aah*," said Miri and Britta, startling away from the window.

"Spying, huh?" said Peder, peering through the glass. "Hm, if you find this sort of action fascinating, I saw a couple of rocks back there you might be eager to gape at." But he leaned closer to the window, Miri and Britta joining him.

Felissa began speaking, Steffan answering, and after a few minutes the four reunited siblings seemed to be having a real conversation. Miri thought it was going pretty well until Steffan rose suddenly and left the room.

"What's he doing?" Miri asked.

"It looks like," said Peder, "he's coming out—"

"Britta?" Steffan called.

Britta, Peder, and Miri stumbled away from the window, tripping over shrubs and hobbling back onto the stone garden path. They began to stroll as if that was what they'd been up to from the beginning.

"Um, yes? Steffan? Over here," said Britta.

"Britta, I want to take my sisters out for a ride." His eager gestures reminded Miri of a small boy she knew on Mount Eskel and how excited he'd get whenever he'd talk about soup. "They've never seen the market or the Delegation House or the Opera House. Or anything really! Come with us? Astrid especially was interested in the river bridges."

The five went touring Asland in a carriage till the sun

set and then again all the next day. By the third day, Sus stayed behind because she'd discovered the palace had a library too and wanted to write Kaspar long letters about everything she was reading. Felissa was a little over-whelmed and preferred to keep inside linder walls. She sat with the queen in her receiving room, where some-times they spoke and sometimes just watched the fire, their shoulders touching.

But Steffan and Britta continued to spend most of each day with Astrid.

"What do they talk about?" Miri asked Britta one afternoon when her friend stayed behind to join Miri in the solarium. Miri was keeping as immobile as possible because the palace physician would not approve her travel home till her bones knit back together.

"Everything!" said Britta. "I can't believe I didn't real-ize she was his twin sister the instant I met her. Their expressions, the lilt in their voices, their eyes! They get that same stern expression that makes them look angry when they're only thoughtful, and that same little smile and giggle when they think they're being clever."

"If Steffan had been raised in a swamp," Miri said, "I bet he'd be a champion caiman hunter."

Peder went each morning to Gus's workshop to carve stone because too many idle hours made him itchy and cross-eyed. But he returned to the palace before dinner to sit with Miri and talk and eat. And each night before sleep, she held her linder hawk and quarry-spoke to Marda, all happy memories, her way of saying hello, I miss you, I'll be home soon. She no longer doubted that the hawk could somehow echo quarry-speech all the way home.

She could not communicate complicated messages. She was unable to tell Marda about the note she'd received from Timon, saying that it had been his pleasure to help her escape and he would not be bothering her with a visit after all. That in fact the commerce official had let his father know that Mount Eskel was no longer for sale. Those specific words Miri could not send, but at least she tried to communicate hope.

One bright spring morning when a servant brought Miri a letter in a weather-beaten envelope, she dared to hope it was from Marda, but this she never could have guessed.

> *Miri,*
> > *The widow Lussi said yes.*
> > *I plan to bag two caimans for our wedding feast. You*
> *are invited.*
> > > *Dogface*

Miri replied.

Dogface,

Congratulations to you and Lussi. I wish I could attend, but I am going home. I have sent Fat Hofer coins. Please help him build himself a house. And please watch over him. I think you will. You are no bandit, Dogface. You are a Lesser Alvan.

Miri

On their last night in Asland, Miri and Peder thought to have a simple meal in the garden but a servant fetched them to a feast with the royal family.

For three courses, the silence was broken only by the clatter of dishes and clicks of forks against plates. Steffan and Britta whispered to each other. King Bjorn stared at his food, still avoiding the eyes of his daughters. Felissa and Queen Sabet often reached out to each other—a hand on a wrist, a lean, a pat on the shoulder. Sus was reading a book she tried to hide on her lap. Miri dissected a roasted fish from its bones. It was dripping with a rich butter sauce, but Miri found herself craving fish fresh from the swamp, plain and mild and infused with brine.

"So . . . ," said Miri. "Did I ever tell you all about the time Peder got tangled up in so many goat leads he fell face-first in the stream?"

"Great story, definitely tell that one," said Peder,

"after I tell them about how you used to take off all your clothes and run naked through the village—"

"For the last time, I was three years old!"

Steffan stood up. He seemed to scowl with anger, but Miri guessed he only meant to be serious.

Without preamble he declared, "Britta and I are in agreement. Astrid is your firstborn. I am not the crown prince. She is the crown princess."

Peder laughed one short, delighted laugh.

"What?" said Astrid.

Sus shut her book and looked up with interest.

"Steffan—" the king sputtered.

"We are in agreement," Steffan insisted. "I am stepping down. Astrid was born to the crown."

"It's all right, Steffan," said Astrid. "You don't need to give up the crown for me."

"No, it's not all right, sister," said Steffan. "And I'm not trying to undo years of neglect through one grand act. This is simply what should happen."

Sus nodded thoughtfully. Felissa and Queen Sabet were holding hands.

Steffan began to pace, his arms behind his back, reminding Miri of a master tutor before his class.

"This is not the same kingdom that was torn apart by civil war under Queen Katarina. Before Stora invaded, we were in the middle of a peaceful revolution. We are becoming a nation, commoner delegates joining the nobility. The common people have a voice. They will speak. And what do you think will happen when you announce that a previously unknown Princess Susanna is marrying King Kaspar? And the people discover there are more princesses? And that one of them is my twin, born first? After centuries of nobles grinding commoners under their heels, who do you think the commoners would rally behind? The pampered and palace-born prince or the princess who was cast off by her own parents?"

Miri found herself nodding. Still, could Danland survive another huge change? She made eye contact with Britta, and Britta smiled. She seemed so sure. And quite possibly relieved.

"This is not your decision to make," said the king. "In such matters, we meet with the chief delegate—"

"You forget, Bjorn," said the queen. "I sent the chief delegate away."

The king stared open-mouthed at his wife, at his son, and then at Miri, as if she somehow had any answers.

"Well, I, for one, think Britta would make an excellent chief delegate," said Miri. "I mean, now that she isn't going to be queen."

"Ooh, good choice," said Peder, taking a big bite of bread. He seemed to be having an excellent time.

"Steffan, you know your duty," the king began.

"I'm telling you, the crown is Astrid's," said Steffan. "I didn't ask for it and neither did she, but that's our lot as royals, isn't it, sister?"

Astrid looked furious, but Miri suspected that, like her brother, she was simply thoughtful.

"Steffan, are you sure?" Astrid asked.

He nodded. "You will be exactly the ruler Danland needs. And I'll be here whenever you need me. We'll figure it out together. Besides, Pa is healthy as a horse. He'll live for years."

The king coughed. "They're speculating about my death now?"

Astrid stood up. She took a deep breath. And she nodded.

Felissa stood too, as if in show of support, and Sus sprang to her feet. Miri could not help standing either, with nervous excitement and surprise and joy. Peder joined her, and Britta and the queen. And they all looked at one another, standing around the dining table and not really sure why except that it felt right.

The king stared from his seat.

"My older brother was supposed to be king," he said. "I would that he hadn't died."

"With all respect to your brother, Your Highness," Miri said, "I've read the journal of your father, and I think that you make a far better king than your brother would have. If I were a historian, I would name you King Bjorn Who Listened. There are far worse honorifics."

The king set down his napkin. Slowly, he stood.

"I've made a lot of mistakes," he said quietly. "But I am listening."

Astrid lifted her glass, and Miri could see her hand was shaking. "To King Bjorn, may he listen, and live, for a very, very, very long time."

Everyone raised their glasses. The king joined them.

"To Astrid," he said. "And Felissa. And Susanna. May they forgive—"

He held his napkin to his eyes.

They all sat again, no one speaking, a lot of looking politely away and napkins employed to wipe eyes and blow noses.

Miri was the first to break the silence.

"Did I ever tell you about the time Peder fell face-first into a steaming pile of goat dung?"

Chapter Twenty-seven

The sky leaps with joyous blue
The sun stews a honeyed brew
The wind yelps with pleasure too
Above me it is spring

New leaves twirl up toward the sun
The frost melts, the snow undone
Rivers swell and grasses run
Below me it is spring

My lungs fill with warming air
My heart beats a silent prayer
My mind loosens all despair
Inside me it is spring

Spring snapped like a burst berry. One morning the timid warmth and leftover scent of winter—rusty, lonely, and chill—just popped. Every day the world was greener, the trees fuller, the flowers brighter. And on

Miri and Peder's journey, every step of the horses, every roll of the carriage wheels seemed to draw even more life out of the world till Miri felt so full of it she thought she might burst too.

Miri much preferred returning home to leaving. Two years before, heartache had throbbed hot and prickly in her chest. Now a cool lightness thrummed, as if every instrument in the king's grand orchestra were pressed together and playing inside her a song of expectation.

Like royalty, Miri and Peder rode in a carriage up the winding mountain road, through the pass, up and up, seemingly making for the clouds themselves. And then the path dropped and the entire village was in view. A few dozen stone houses beyond the chapel, its carved wooden doors so lovingly oiled they caught and twinkled the sunlight.

"There," said Peder.

Miri sucked in a breath. Home looked exactly the same. And yet she felt so different. Perhaps she would not fit in it anymore.

Miri's legs were insisting they could run faster than the horses', trembling and aching for the chance. She leaped out of the carriage.

She had forgotten how to walk on the broken rocks and scree that lined Mount Eskel's path, but in just a few strides, her feet remembered. And she had not known she could run so fast. Peder raced beside her, laughing.

One of Frid's big brothers saw them and turned to shout to the village. People began to pour out of the quarry and houses, dozens and dozens, the entire village from small child to grandmother coming together, waving, calling their names. Her whole, big extended family of friends and neighbors shouting the glad news that Miri and Peder were home.

In front of them all, Marda. Shy Marda who rarely spoke, who kept her gaze down when she walked. Marda was running, her pale hair streaking behind her, her arms out.

"Miri! Miri! You're home, you're here! Miri!"

Yes, Miri could definitely run faster than lowlander horses.

In moments she reached her. They collided together in a hard embrace that sent them both tumbling to the ground, laughing and hugging and crying all at once.

"I heard you," said Marda. "You quarry-spoke and I heard, every day this spring."

And then Pa was there. He picked them both off the ground and hugged them together, his huge arms wrapped around them, squeezing their family together so tightly Miri was certain they would never be apart again.

He put his large hands on Miri's face. "You didn't die," he said, his voice as low and rumbly as a rock slide.

She shook her head.

"I thought you'd died," he said. "My heart felt like you had."

She shook her head again. She could not speak.

"Will you stay? For a good long time at least. Will you stay home?"

She nodded.

Pa hugged her. And then as if he could not contain his happiness, he picked Miri up under her arms and tossed her into the air, as he used to do when she was a small child.

"Pa!" she said. Just because she was short did not mean she should be treated like a child. But secretly she liked to fly from his safe arms up into the huge blue sky.

He did it again. Miri flew.

As soon as Miri gained her feet, she delivered the news.

"Mount Eskel is ours," she said. "The king signed it over—all of it. The village, the quarry, all the land between the pass and the mountain's top. The academy graduates and our children will be the legal land owners. It means no one can take our home away from us, not even the king."

With that news, a spontaneous holiday erupted on the springtime mountain. Gerti fetched her lute, and her father, Os, his three-stringed yipper. Frid danced with her lowlander beau, Sweyn, and Esa danced with Almond, who grinned the whole time. People brought out food and lit a bonfire in the village center.

Miri sat between Pa and Marda, trying to deliver all the news of the past months. A small crowd gathered to hear her stories. She particularly enjoyed retelling the caiman hunt, Dogface's rescue, and Astrid wrestling the gigantic soldier.

Peder joined her with a whisper, "My pa said yes."

No one's mood could stay sour in the village that day.

And so the next morning, Miri and Peder entered the village chapel. Miri was dressed in gifts. A blue silk dress Queen Sabet had sent with her, a jeweled dragon-fly pin the sisters had had made, and gray leather slippers from Britta, so thin and soft they felt like bare feet.

The betrothal ceremony was much simpler than a wedding ceremony. Just a quick exchange of vows, promising each other they would be true during their betrothal year. A year from that date, they could wed.

Miri held Peder's hands in front of their families and friends. And she did not blush when he kissed her.

Peder's ma, Doter, wept. Miri's pa nodded again and again. The ceremony was over, and the villagers returned to the quarry. The hammering and pounding of stone filled the air, as noisy as twenty swamps.

Peder kissed Miri one more time and then went to inspect the cut linder blocks and select a good stone for carving. Miri arranged with his sister Esa to join her in the village school that afternoon to help teach. First she gathered both their families' goats and coaxed them up the hill to graze. She had a book in her apron pocket and a betrothal flower laced around her finger.

Near the quarry, Frid was wiping down the new anvil. Sweyn put a hand on her back and whispered something. Frid laughed. Beyond, the rugged angles of the quarry were busy with workers. Through the ground, the echoes of quarry-speech reached Miri, the villagers talking to one another as they worked.

Lighten the blow.

Strike swiftly.

Aim true.

Peder was examining a stone. Miri caught his eye and waved. He pressed his hand to his heart as if the sight of her made it pound so hard that he had to push it back into his chest. She laughed.

Miri leaned back against the throne of the hill and opened her book. The goats bleated over the new green grass. Above her, the sun burned against the snowy top of Mount Eskel. The golden light blazed around Miri's head like a crown.

Epilogue

The academy was held in a country estate a day's ride outside Asland. The estate's lord had graciously volunteered to remain in his city house for the year and donate his country home for the need. That is, he'd volunteered after the queen, her daughters and son, and Britta, the newly appointed chief delegate, instructed him to do so.

The lush gold-papered drawing room had been emptied of couches and piano. The students sat at individual desks, clay tablets and styluses at the ready. Most kept glancing at the portrait of Princess Astrid hanging at the head of the room. In a year's time, there would be a ball in her honor. Princess Astrid would meet all the students of the academy. She would speak with them and dance with them. And eventually, she would make her choice. The knowledge seemed to hum in the air, exciting anticipation and not a little anxiety.

The door opened. A woman entered. If one word could be applied to her, it was "imposing." She wore all black, her short black hair cut flat on the end like a chisel. Her expression was fierce, her posture so straight she put fence posts to shame.

She looked over her new class—twenty boys, commoners and nobles, each selected by the priests of the creator god to attend the sacred academy.

"Good morning," she said, almost meaning it. "I am Olana Mansdaughter. When I give you permission to speak, you will address me as Tutor Olana. Welcome to the prince academy."

Acknowledgments

My travels with Miri began in 2003. Over a decade later, I feel quite nostalgic as I bring them to an end. These books would not exist in any form without the wisdom and inspiration from my editor, Victoria Wells Arms, and my husband, Dean Hale.

It takes a village to raise a book, so a hearty thanks to the village at Bloomsbury, including Hali Baumstein, Cindy Loh, Donna Mark, Lizzy Mason, Beth Eller, Linette Kim, Cristina Gilbert, Erica Barmash, Melissa Kavonic, and Patricia McHugh, as well as to Amy Lu Jameson, Barry Goldblatt, Tricia Ready, Jared Hess, and Max Hale. Kisses for Ann Cannon, Ally Condie, and Ann Dee Ellis for your support and snacks. As always, much love to my hometown bookstore, The King's English, and to booksellers and librarians everywhere who match up readers with just the right books.

For help creating Lesser Alva, I pulled on a visit to the Reed Islands of Lake Titicaca and *The Marsh Arabs* by Wilfred Thesiger.

I feel so grateful that I got to travel with Miri across three books. Profound thanks to my readers whose encouragement and patronage allowed that journey. I'm honored that Miri might accompany you on your own.